Barrier

THE OTHER HORIZONS TRILOGY:
BOOK TWO

Barrier

The Other Horizons Trilogy: Book Two

Mary Victoria Johnson

LODESTONE
BOOKS

Winchester, UK
Washington, USA

First published by Lodestone Books, 2018
Lodestone Books is an imprint of John Hunt Publishing Ltd., No. 3 East St., Alresford,
Hampshire SO24 9EE, UK
office1@jhpbooks.net
www.johnhuntpublishing.com

For distributor details and how to order please visit the 'Ordering' section on our website.

Text copyright: Mary Victoria Johnson 2017

ISBN: 978 1 78535 428 1
978 1 78535 429 8 (ebook)
Library of Congress Control Number: 2016931747

A CIP catalogue record for this book is available from the British Library.

Design: Stuart Davies

Printed and bound by CPI Group (UK) Ltd, Croydon, CR0 4YY, UK

We operate a distinctive and ethical publishing philosophy in
all areas of our business, from our global network of authors to
production and worldwide distribution.

To Clara

I'm proud to be your sister too. Keep shining!

Other Books by Mary Victoria Johnson

Boundary, The Other Horizons Trilogy – Book One
(Lodestone Books, 978-1-78279-918-4)

PART ONE

Chapter One

There were few things that I was certain of these days, but this was one of them: trains were a nightmare. The headmistress of the school, whom I had accidentally kept referring to as 'Master', had personally escorted me to the station in fear of my reaction, anticipating the worst and getting it. I'd thrown a screaming fit when the engine had come puffing through the station, spewing great clouds of plumed smoke everywhere so that I could barely see nor breathe, wheels shrieking in protest as they skidded to a halt, people jostling left and right.

People. Another thing I didn't like. I'd only ever met eight others before escaping Boundary, and suddenly having to cope with hundreds was disorienting to say the least. Everywhere I went there was a never-ending wave of new faces, new voices, and new names. The oddest part was that I was as much a stranger to them as they were to me. I'd never been a stranger to anybody before. There was something extremely lonely about being unknown, and about speaking to people who hadn't the slightest idea who I was, and would forget me by the next day.

The school had helped, to begin with. Nobody believed my story of Boundary, and I learned quickly enough that trying to persuade everyone that I was telling the truth got me nowhere. Eventually, they decided the best thing to do would be to send me to a boarding school, until I managed to 'unscramble my poor, confused mind'. That was how they phrased it. Even in this world, people regarded me as an idiot.

The girls had initially been very nice to me, but after a while, they took my constant ignorance as a plea for attention and began turning away. Anyway, anybody who woke up almost every night screaming about a fire and a non-existent boy named Fred wasn't considered socially desirable.

Then one day, the headmistress told me that the school was being shut down due to lack of funding, or something to that effect. I wasn't eighteen, and clearly not capable of living alone. I had no family. She told me I was to live with her sister-in-law on a farm, not too far from the school. That had been that. I'd packed my spare dress and caught the next train out of town, still not being sure what a farm was, or what one was expected to do on it.

People. People. People. Everywhere. Noise, noise, people, strange smells, people, noise...it never went away.

I'd been lucky enough to find a seat by the window, enabling me to turn away from the crowds and chaos of the third-class carriage to focus on the scenery outside.

Countryside whizzed past me at incredible speeds, a blur of open fields, hedges, country roads, and clumps of trees. We had passed few towns since departure, and every time we did, I purposely turned my head away. It scared me too much, thinking about just how many people there were out there.

I was fascinated by the country, which served as a good distractor. In the boarding school, it had been easy to pretend the outside didn't exist and that I was simply living in another version of Boundary with lots more girls and no Ripping. Ripping was a form of magic, which I did not care to remember, from my old life at Boundary. I hadn't ventured farther than the school grounds whenever I could help it, only visiting the town itself once or twice in all my time there.

The countryside was different from the town. Though I was still irrationally afraid of all animals, I found the sprawling fields and rolling hills mesmerizing. It was hard to believe that the land carried on for farther than one could walk, with the restriction being only how far you were willing to go. No boundaries. Nothing to keep you locked into one place—one estate.

Boundary. Penny, Tressa, Avery, Lucas, and Fred. Missing them was a physical ache in my chest, and not purely one of sadness, but one of guilt. Guilt that I'd escaped in Penny's place, and that I could do nothing to help my five friends. Guilt that here I was, standing on a train speeding miles and miles away from them.

The train blew its whistle, jolting me right out of my thoughts, slowing down into a small station. My good mood evaporated instantaneously. Now I'd have to navigate the hordes of people and remember what it was I was supposed to do, and then endure a car ride.

Lovely.

The conductor ushered the small crowd of departing passengers towards a door, where we stepped down a single step onto the platform. A few people hopped on, and what seemed like mere minutes later, steam filled the station and the train began chugging onward again.

For a moment, I stood amongst the moving people in a daze, watching them rush around me. The headmistress had given me clear instructions: go to the main gate and ask for Julia Pearson if I couldn't find anyone waiting. But what was a main gate?

Just like that, I found myself alone on a deserted village station, little suitcase in hand and tears embarrassingly blurring my eyesight. I didn't like being left alone without someone telling me what to do.

There was a fence on the other side of the railway tracks, this world's idea of a boundary. On the other side, behind me, there was a brick wall. An array of posters that were plastered to it caught my eye, and I began walking closer.

"Miss?" A young boy, no more than fourteen, dressed in a porter's uniform came hurrying towards me. "You need a hand with anything?"

"The main gate," I said immediately, my voice coming out sounding slightly unsure of what I was saying.

"Just this way, Miss. You wouldn't happen to be Evelyn, would you? Only there's a woman asking after you at the front, says her name is Julia Pearson."

I nodded, relieved and tore myself away from the posters to

follow him. I'd seen most of them before anyway. There was no escaping the war.

War. That, as it turned out, was the major setback of this new age.

Chapter Two

"...So I says, 'You can go after your glory all you want, Billy, but the real important stuff is done right 'ere at home.' 'E went anyway of course, stubborn mule like 'e is, but Mama said that in 'er eyes, we was both doin' as noble a thing as we could. 'Land service,' she says, 'is bloody 'ard work but it's what keeps England chuggin' away durin' these times. Nothin' more respectable for a girl to do.' Billy can argue all 'e wants, but there ain't no denyin' it."

"Kitty Rogers," Julia Pearson said through clenched teeth, knuckles white against the steering wheel. "If you don't stop this ridiculous nattering, then when Evelyn vomits again, I shall personally ensure it is all over you. For the love of God, *shut up*."

"Sorry, Aunt Jule." Kitty beamed before turning to gawp out of the dirt-encrusted window.

Julia was a thirty-something woman who looked about ten years older. She was robust woman with almost colourless brown hair pulled into a knot at the base of her freckled neck. Mr Pearson, she hastened to inform me, was attending a farmer's conference, and would be back to help us soon.

There had been another girl in the car. Kitty Rogers, niece of Julia, easily surpassed Avery as the most irritating person I had ever met. Her accent was a different one from the country drawl altogether, much rougher and harder to understand. All I knew was that she came from some large city, and like me, would be working on the farm. She must have been around my age, perhaps eighteen or nineteen, with a round, cheery face and chestnut hair curled in exactly the way I disliked. She was very tall and somewhat lanky, but unlike the girls at school, didn't seem to mind that I was obviously prettier. A quick appraisal of me hadn't been followed by the usual glare of envy, but rather a friendly crooked-tooth grin. If she stopped talking, I might have also found myself liking Kitty.

As for the car...it lacked any of the smoothness I had grown to enjoy with trains, constantly spluttering and bouncing over every pothole and tipping around every horrendous country lane corner. Unlike the vehicle that had driven me from the school to the station, this one lacked an overhead roof, making it difficult to hear properly over the howling wind. The windows and visor stopped it from ruining my hair completely, but I was still very uncomfortable, and more than a little green. Twice Julia had stopped the car so I could be sick in the bushes.

"So is it true that we ain't supposed to ask you about where you came from before the school...your family, or anythin' about your past?" Kitty asked me, turning back around in her seat to face me. "That's what it said in the letter your 'eadmistress sent. Bit strange, I thought, but then people do all kinds of undercover stuff nowadays."

I blew my nose delicately so that I wouldn't have to reply. Unfortunately, even though I fussed for much longer than was necessary, Kitty was still waiting for me to answer.

"It's nothing like that." I sighed, feeling the bile rise in my throat as we skidded around another bend. "Honestly, you'd be disappointed."

"Nah, I'm always game for a story." She grinned. "So is it like, you *can't* tell, or you don't want to?"

"Both," I replied truthfully. Even someone as open-minded as Kitty couldn't possibly comprehend what Boundary had been without thinking me crazy. I was only glad the headmistress had taken the time to write that letter.

"Maybe one day you'll have to let me in on it," she suggested. "Though I warn you, I ain't good at keepin' secrets. Tell me, an' everyone will know. There was this one time where my sister asked me not to tell this boy she loved 'im, but I just couldn't hold it in when 'e came around and anyway, to cut a long story short, she wouldn't talk to me for days, an' even when he asked 'er out she said no out of stubbornness. D'you have anyone special you're leavin'?"

"No," I replied, much too quickly.

Julia flicked me a sympathetic look in the mirror, probably assuming that I'd fallen for a dashing young man at school who had left me for the army, and I was too upset to talk. I wasn't going to correct her.

I leaned my forehead against the door, and then pulled away as the intense vibrations increased my headache. I wanted nothing more than for the torture to stop. What was wrong with walking, anyway? Too old-fashioned?

"I'm surprised." Kitty cocked an eyebrow with a playful smile. "Pretty thing like you."

"Tell me about the farm," I suggested, eyeing my feet with intense concentration, finding that if I focused on something hard enough the motion sickness subsided slightly.

"Well, I've only been 'ere a couple o' times as a kid," she began, enthusiastic now I had actually asked her to speak instead of giving abrupt answers. "But it's really quite lovely. Not too big, which is lucky for us since we only got mostly girls workin', but still lovely. When I was little, we used to…"

I closed my ears to her. Overhead, a flock of birds soared up against the blue October sky, as graceful and effortless as the clouds themselves. It was relaxing watching them—until the car swerved around another tight bend and I lost them over the skeletal branches of the overhanging trees. I gasped suddenly, and was forced to hang out of the side of the car to heave, but nothing came out as my stomach was already empty.

"You all right, Ev?" Kitty patted my back.

"Evelyn," I corrected weakly, embarrassed.

"Don't like shortened names, then? That's all right. I hated it when Billy called me Kit. Sounds like a boy's name, don't it?"

"We're here!" Julia announced, turning sharply up a dusty track, then throwing on the brakes and opening the door. "Home sweet home."

When my feet first made contact with the ground, they felt as if they were made of jelly. I took a few shaky steps and nearly fell, vowing never to travel by car ever, ever, ever again.

"Everyone!" Kitty shouted, cupping her hands around her mouth. "Come meet Evelyn!"

My eyes widened in shock. My hair was messed up by the wind, cheeks blotchy, blouse dusty, and headache ruthless, so much for good first impressions.

To calm my nerves, I looked at the house itself. It was smaller than the various barns I could see dotting the sprawling landscape, with thick, whitewashed walls and a higgledy-piggledy roof that seemed to be composed of slate simply chucked on by children. The windows were covered in Xs made of tape, for whatever reason, and the air stunk of animals.

"Mummy!" voices called from inside, as shrilly cheerful as Kitty's without the city accent.

Several shapes emerged from the dust, of all shapes and sizes. I nodded shyly at the seven figures that were staring at me with overt curiosity.

Julia gave them each a hug, and then turned to me taking my elbow and pulling me forwards to meet them.

"I'm James," a gap-toothed boy announced, extending a hand for me to shake. He had Julia's flat hair colour, but his eyes were much brighter. "I'm glad you're here, 'cause it's my birthday next week and I want lots of people here. I'm going to be ten!"

I flashed a wan smile of congratulations, and then Julia dragged me on to the next people.

Two girls, about fourteen or fifteen (twins I guessed), inspected me cautiously. One was noticeably taller, with widely spaced brows and a pretty, fair complexion. The other had a curvier figure, but plainer looks, and curly brown hair falling in waves down to her waist.

The taller girl spoke first. "Hi. I'm Anna. This here is Harriet, but don't expect her to talk too much, she's painfully shy. It's nice to meet you."

Harriet shot her sister a dirty look, crossed her arms and blushed.

Next I was introduced to three older men: Pat, Gregory, and Charlie, who was Julia's father.

"We're the only farmhands left now," he explained in a loud whisper, as if letting me into a secret. "Peter, Robbie, Jack, Douglas...all gone to fight."

They weren't, however, the only men there.

"Andrew." The boy—well, almost a man, really—grinned, eyes scanning my face in slight amusement. "The big brother."

I nodded, confused. I had been under the impression all the fit males had gone to enlist in the army, yet here was this young man who couldn't have been more than nineteen.

Freckles dusted his face, painting him as one of Julia's children. His sandy hair blew in front of his green, laughing eyes. Strong looking, he had the build of a worker, and features that were almost handsome—the picture of a model soldier.

"It's going to be hard without the boys, but we'll manage." Julia smiled, as we all turned to go inside. "Thank you ever so much for volunteering to help—you and Kitty both. Because we're not a proper—I mean, big—farm, they tend to overlook us when recruiting."

I wasn't listening. Andrew, chatting in a low voice to Anna, was walking in a very peculiar fashion, as if one leg kept getting stuck on the ground and was weighing him down—a definite and severe limp.

"What's wrong with Andrew?"

I felt Julia's arm tense, but her smile did not waver as she answered, "He had an accident about a year ago. Nearly lost his leg, though to be brutally honest, I can't say I'm not relieved to have one of my sons home from this war. Just...don't bring it up around him. It's a touchy subject."

"I'm sorry."

"No, no, you had to ask. Come, the sun's going down, and you're probably hungry."

Inside, the house was easily the most cramped yet cosy space I had ever set eyes on.

The entire downstairs could not have been much larger than our common room inside Boundary. The thick walls were criss-crossed with timber beams, the low doorways causing Gregory and Andrew to bend their heads to avoid scraping them. In the kitchen, the quarry-tiled floor was worn by many generations of feet. The furniture was basic, with a pine Welsh dresser displaying an assortment of odd dishes, and two worn armchairs sat on either side of an old cooking range. A ceramic sink with a wooden draining board stood in one corner, while in another the narrow staircase wound upwards to a dark second floor.

What drew my eyes was a handmade table that seemed to swallow all remaining floor area, for upon it was a delicious supper that smelled simply heavenly. Everyone sat down around it, chatting, waiting for Julia and I to sit down before beginning.

"Cor, what we got 'ere, Aunt Jule?" Kitty asked, nearly drooling as she surveyed the steaming pots. "I ain't eaten properly in days. Food's gettin' so bloody scarce in the cities."

"No swearing at the table please, Kitty," Julia scolded. "We've got roast parsnips, pork, and the garden veggies. I've got a pie in the oven for pudding too."

I sat down, awkwardly wedged between Charlie and Anna on a stool that seemed seconds away from shattering underneath me. Kitty was opposite, stuffing carrots into her mouth before they even touched the plate, rather like how Penny... No. I wasn't there anymore. I wouldn't lose myself in pretending.

"Harriet, could you flick the light on please?" Julia glanced up from spooning peas onto James's plate. "Dark at six o'clock. Winter isn't waiting for the war to end."

I flinched as the bulb above our heads whined before flickering on, casting a steady light about the place. Bulbs weren't as homely as candles, also the science behind electricity blew my mind, but I understood that it must be much safer than having small fires everywhere.

"It won't be much longer until we're short on food too," Andrew mused. "We'll be reduced to curds and cabbage by Christmas, that's what they say. Our food stocks are running low."

"I hate cabbage," James offered.

"Cabbage don't taste like nothin'." Kitty winced, prodding her pork thoughtfully. "Can't really like it or dislike it."

"I'm not worried about *you* fussing, Kitty," Andrew chortled. "You'd eat a gallon of uncooked worms if that was all that was available. It's old picky-pants over there, and our new schoolgirl who I think might struggle a bit when we're stuck chewing roots."

I felt my face burn red. Staring at my plate, feeling glances ricochet off me from all over the table, that familiar longing to be amongst my old friends again resurfaced with vengeance.

"Don't listen to him," Anna whispered. "He's just trying to get your attention."

Andrew's cheeks burned a bright red, and he didn't speak for the rest of the meal.

"More parsnips, Evelyn?" Julia asked.

"Actually, Mrs Pearson, I'm quite tired from the journey today. Would you mind if I turned in for the night? The food really is lovely, but I'm nearly falling asleep at the table," I admitted, hoping I wasn't sounding too overly polite. I meant it, of course, but I couldn't forget the mimicry of the girls at my schools. 'Sickly sweet', they'd jeered.

Julia stood up, wiped the corners of her mouth with a napkin, and excused herself. I did the same, legs shaking a bit as I stood up.

"You know I was only joking," Andrew muttered as I rounded the table to the staircase. He leaned forward so that only I could

12

hear.

I gave a stiff nod, saying nothing, wondering again how I was appearing to them.

Up the creaking staircase, I was shown a tiny room that was more like a cave than bedchamber. It had a peculiar window that touched the floor and rose to about knee-length, so that one would have to kneel to see out of it. With only a wardrobe for furniture bedsides the bunk bed, it felt claustrophobic compared to the hall-like room I had slept in during my school time.

"It's all we can squeeze you into, I'm afraid," Julia said, reading my expression. "This used to be where Robbie and Peter slept...but you'll share with Kitty now. She'll chat until her breath runs out, but her heart is in the right place."

"You've a lovely family."

"Yes. I'm lucky. Anyway, enough of the chat...I'll be serving breakfast at six o'clock on the dot so we can start our chores nice and early. You can start out doing mainly domestics in the house with me. We'll see how the boys do outside before we assign positions. Besides, the surveyor, Mr Farrington, is coming tomorrow so it might postpone things a little bit."

"Is there much dirty work to do then?" I wrinkled my nose, thinking of the animal smell and muddy fields outside.

"Oh, yes. Even in the autumn and winter." Julia laughed, and bent down pulling the curtains for me so that the room was thrown into a dim, pinkish light. "Bathroom is the third door to your left. And remember you can only fill the bath tub with a maximum of five inches of hot water. Goodnight!"

I waved her away with a tired smile, exhaling slowly when the door shut. It was going to be a long, long war.

I changed into my nightdress, and tiptoed over to the bathroom with my little soap bag. It was a freezing room, tiny and slightly mouldy around the edges, so I didn't linger for too long.

As I tied curlers into my hair, jumping slightly as Kitty

pounded on the door, a peculiar thought floated through my drowsy mind.

Farrington?

Somewhere in the darker recesses of my memory, an alarm bell was ringing.

No, it couldn't be. I was overreacting. By the time I'd jumped into bed, I'd pushed the thought straight out of mind, deciding it was nothing more than a coincidence

Chapter Three

Beatrix, our housekeeper, had always told us that we could sleep in until whenever we wanted, as our bodies knew exactly how much rest we needed. Being unceremoniously awakened by Kitty's rough drawl wasn't exactly the best way to wake up, and I felt my head pound as all the events of the past day came rushing back to me.

"That ain't funny, Anna! It's bloody freezin', I could o' gone into shock, you know!"

"Shut up, Kitty! If Mum catches you swearing when James can hear you, she'll have your guts for garters!"

"Stuck-up cow," Kitty snarled, slamming the door behind her as she stomped into my room. She had flung a towel around herself, her hair lying in soaking wet rattails, and her teeth chattering in her jaw. "Could o' told me she'd just wasted all the water, but no, just stood there watchin' whilst I nearly die of—hey, aren't you awake yet, Evelyn? Breakfast is going to be finished if you don't hurry up."

I rubbed the sleep from my eyes, shivering as feeling crept into my toes. Peeling away the blanket, I swung my feet onto the carpet and forced myself to stand up. What I saw nearly made me jump back in bed; Kitty had dropped her towel and was rooting around in her suitcase for a dressing gown, stark naked.

"Sorry." She shrugged, seeing my mortified expression. "Want me to get changed in the bathroom?"

I nodded stiffly, squeaking, "I think that would be best, if you don't mind."

She left with a handful of clothing and a hairbrush, and I quickly shut the door behind her.

That was another thing that had been difficult to adjust to. Inside Boundary, we'd worn corsets and full skirts and collars that had covered our necks. We'd had gloves and bonnets, petticoats and stockings, and the boys had worn waistcoats, jackets and proper trousers. Here, I wore shirts (*shirts!*) tucked into knee-length skirts with stockings and cardigans. Propriety just didn't matter quite so much as it had, which took a lot of adjusting to.

Behind the curtains, the sun had risen slowly over the rolling horizon, bringing with it a soft glow that lit all the frost-encrusted trees and fields with gold. Everything was fresh, new, and peaceful, and for a moment the scene mesmerized me, having only woken up to two different views in my entire life. There was no better distraction.

After brushing my black curls into position and fastening all my buttons, I opened the door again. Harriet was standing outside the bathroom, a glassy expression on her face. Anna was bickering with Kitty inside over a hairbrush, and from downstairs I could hear Andrew arguing with Julia, and James shouting something over and over again.

"It's a madhouse," Harriet whispered, not looking at me and directing her voice to the wall. I paused, unsure if I was meant to respond. "They're not happy you're here. You're making them angry."

"You mean your family?" I frowned, confused. "I...I was under the impression Julia wanted me to come. I thought she needed the help."

"No. I mean the *Others*," Harriet corrected, blinking rapidly as if there was something in her eye. "They're not here now, but they were watching you last night. They were here a few minutes ago. They aren't happy you're here."

"Who are the Others?" I asked, a shiver creeping down my spine. "I don't understand."

Harriet opened her mouth, finally turning to me, but at that moment the bathroom door opened and Anna came storming out, fuming.

"...Not like she lives here, self-entitled— Harriet? Are you all right?"

"They visited Evelyn a few minutes ago," Harriet explained. "You know, the Others. Don't tell me I'm crazy again, I'm trying to help."

"I'm going to have some breakfast," I offered awkwardly, seeing Anna's face fall even further. "Thank you for your help, Harriet."

I felt the twins' eyes on my back as I crept down the stairs. Harriet had a point: what sort of madhouse had I walked into?

The smell of fried eggs greeted me as I walked into the kitchen, and thankfully everyone had settled their arguments and had sat back down. Julia gave me a tight, but still warm smile, flipping an egg onto a plate and setting it down on the seat between Andrew and James. The older men were out in the fields already, I learned, preparing for the surveyor.

"Hello, Evelyn. Sleep well?"

"Yes. Well, I got a very interesting wakeup. But the room is perfect, thank you."

"Harriet?" Julia asked, amused. "Ignore her. She's looking for attention, has been ever since Robbie and Peter left for war and I...anyway, just ignore her. She'll try to scare you by acting all spooky, but there's no substance behind what she says and she'll go back to normal once she realizes you're not falling for it."

"Thanks." I offered a forced smile. "I guess I'm just on edge already about trying not to mess up here."

"Oh, you won't mess up, not with Mum organizing." Andrew chuckled. "She's determined to prove to the men that she's capable of controlling everything."

"Until your father gets home, at least," Julia reminded him, gently pushing a fidgety James outside. "Are you all right to work outside today, Andrew? Greg, Pat, and Charlie are going to do a general tidy up for when the surveyor arrives, and the girls won't be able to tend to the animals by themselves. Get James to feed the chickens, then—"

"Cows, horses, and pigs. I know, Mum." Andrew laughed,

limping over to the sink. "I suppose you'll want me to show Evelyn the ropes?"

"No, we'll start her off inside for now. I need help doing the chores."

"All right. I'll go get the girls." He seemed a little disappointed.

I waited until everyone had left, then turned to Julia. "Can I help you with anything?"

"Dishes first. I can wash if you dry."

She handed me a tea towel that smelled strongly of milk, and began piling plates onto the counter in front of me. I stared at them for a few minutes, trying to figure out what I was supposed to be doing, and then tentatively began to wipe them with the towel so that the bubbles vanished and they looked somewhat dry.

"You realize you have to do each plate individually," Julia pointed out, and I couldn't tell what the expression was on her face: either amusement or disbelief. She picked up the first plate, and showed me the puddle of water trapped between the stack.

Blushing furiously, appalled that I couldn't do something that simple without help, I began drying them properly. It was a tedious task, and twice they nearly slipped out of my hands, but after probably half an hour I was rewarded with a pile of clean, dry dishes all ready for their next use.

"I've finished!" I called, pleased, wiping my hands and even going so far as to put them away in the correct cupboards.

"Perfect!" Julia exclaimed from upstairs. "Now we'll just have to work at speed. I'm just cleaning the bathroom. It looks like a whale was splashing around in here after those girls! Then I'm going to pop to town and get some things for lunch, so would you be a sweetheart and put the laundry out to dry?"

"Hang out the..." I trailed off, trying to figure out what that could possibly mean, yet too proud to ask.

Julia rushed past me down the stairs, pinning her hair up as she went. "I'm going to have to make a rule about bathroom cleanliness," she muttered, pulling on a coat and grabbing a handbag. "Do you know what you're doing, then? Or do you want me to show you quickly before I go?"

"I'm fine," I lied, cursing myself the second I'd said the words.

Julia raised an eyebrow, studying me for a moment before buckling her shoes and plodding outside towards the car.

I waited until the drone of the engine had grown faint before collapsing into a nearby chair, running a hand through my hair. What was I *doing* here? I didn't know how to do anything, including handle my host family, and on the first day had succeeded in making a fool of myself. I felt stupid, I felt useless, and I had no idea what in the world 'putting out the laundry' entailed.

Don't cry. Don't cry. Don't cry.

I wiped my eyes with the back of my hand, going back to step one. Laundry was dirty clothes that had been washed — that much I did know. As for putting it outside, there was only one place that she could be referring to.

I found the hamper of neatly folded, damp clothing on the cellar stairs, so I hauled it over to the side door, even though my back felt as if it was going to snap from the weight. From the doorway, I could see it was warming up outside, with the frost already beginning to melt thanks to the morning sun, but I couldn't help shivering under my thin cardigan. In front of me, there was nothing but a muddy garden and beyond it acres upon acres of barren farmland. I could hear the others chatting around the other side of the house, where the animal barns and paddocks were, so I was glad to be out of sight around this side.

I took an uncertain step, and the mud squelched as my foot made contact. Other foot, right foot, left foot…it was painstaking work, trying to wade through the sticky mud and carry the hamper at the same time, and by the time I reached the yard again, I was wheezing from lack of breath and had sloshed dirt all the way up the back of my skirt.

Right. I did a quick scan to try and figure out where I was supposed to put the clothes, and my eyes were drawn to a thin wire pulled tightly between the side of the house and a concrete post about ten feet away. If I hung the clothes over this wire in a certain way, then maybe, just maybe, they would dry from exposure to this crisp air.

There was a worn paper bag in the hamper, containing a multitude of wooden clip things, so I moved them out of the way before pulling out the garments one by one. They were damp and heavy under my fingers, and when I reach up to hang them over the wire, they bunched up in a way that would keep them wet for ages.

On my tiptoes, not quite tall enough to reach the wire with ease, I flung the next shirt over the wire and pulled it flat. I felt stretched, and a little dizzy from having my head tilted back for so long. To make matters worse, there were another thirty pieces to go.

"This is why people have housekeepers," I muttered with a touch of bitterness. Boundary truly was a world away.

Minute by agonizing minute, I pulled out the clothes on the line in what I hoped was the proper fashion. It took me over an hour to empty the entire basket onto the line, and towards the end everything became rather clumped up. I wiped my hair from my face, turning over the hamper so that I could sit down upon it for a minute.

My head fell into my hands, my eyes closed, and for a moment I think I dozed off.

Then a dull splat shattered through my dreams, and I snapped bolt upright. Every single item had slipped off, and was now lying in the defrosted muck, ruined. *Every. Single. One.*

"Oh no," I moaned, jumping up and running over to where the largest pile was. Julia was going to be so mad!

My foot caught in the mud, and I tripped over before even realizing what was going on. I gave a small gasp of disgust, jumping back up again and wiping the soggy dirt on my apron.

Mud had saturated the clothes, now completely encrusted and dried in crinkled positions.

I twirled a strand of hair as I always did when I got frustrated, then jerked my hand away when I realized it was covered with sludge from the ground. I was filthy.

"Come on, come one," I begged the clothing, as if it would all spring back up on the line again, clean as before. "Please!"

I picked up a pair of trousers, trying to convince myself that a simple brushing off would do the trick

"Urgh!" I squealed in annoyance. I flung them back onto the ground and crossed my arms, wincing as the mud began seeping through my dress.

Then I realized I was being watched.

This day just kept getting better.

"You know, Evelyn, talking to clothing has got to be a sign of madness," Andrew observed, a hint of a smile curling upon his lips. "Just because Harriet has imaginary friends, it doesn't mean you need to compete with her."

"Oh, very funny," I snapped, humiliated and exasperated. "I didn't...these..."

He raised a fair eyebrow as my words trailed off into an irritated silence, limping over to retrieve the paper bag from the muck. "Do you know what these are?"

I listened to the wooden things clink together as he shook them, racking my brain for similar objects that they had used at the school. I drew a blank, and admitted in a small voice, "No."

I folded my arms and waited for an explanation, but Andrew stood there frozen for a moment, speechless. It was then I realized that he had been asking sarcastically, and had assumed that I knew what those commonplace items had been. Ashamed, I turned around and began picking the dirty clothes up off the ground so I wouldn't have to face his judgement.

"Evelyn," he said finally, and I was surprised by the softness in his voice. "I'm sorry. I didn't realize you...I suppose you never had use for pegs at the boarding school, did you?"

I shook my head, focussing on the clothing. He must have thought I was a useless, spoiled little princess. Perhaps he wouldn't have been wrong.

"What about your mother? Didn't she help you with these things?" he pressed, sounding genuinely intrigued but still careful, as if I was a wrong word away from crying, which, honestly, I probably was.

"I don't know who my mother is," I replied in a hoarse whisper. "I've never seen my parents. I don't even know their names."

There were no more clothes to distract me, and I was forced to stand up. I averted my eyes from his, afraid I would see that awful patronizing look that I had grown so used to.

Please don't ask me. Don't ask about my past.

"Well, for a start, we need to get those clothes clean before we hang them back up again," he decided briskly, and my head snapped up in surprise. "Most of them we can probably just shake the dirt off, but the ones which fell in the puddle need washing again. I'll get Kitty to give us a hand, then I'll show you how to use pegs to pin them to the line."

"Thank you?" I phrased it as a question, unsure of why he was taking time out of his own chores to help me. "Will Julia not be angry you're not doing your own job?"

"The old boys have finished with the field, so they helped us tend to the animals. Besides, this has all the makings of an emergency." Andrew winked, jogging as fast as his injured leg would allow back into the house, hollering for Kitty.

They both emerged a few minutes later, hauling a great tin basin of lukewarm water between them.

"Stars above, that's 'eavy," Kitty grunted, massaging her sore fingers. "You got everythin' dirty again? Aunt Jule shouldn't be back for another hour, so we'll 'elp sort this mess. Didn't spare no expense in gettin' things mucky, did ya?"

"Finished?" Andrew rolled his eyes. "All right. So, Evelyn, all we're going to do is rinse off the dirt instead of going through the whole procedure, but if Mum ever asks you to help her do the washing, you'll need to use much hotter water with soap. So all we're going to do now, is Kitty will rinse, I'll wring, and you can peg everything to the line."

I stared between him and the tin basin as if he was speaking foreign language.

"Anybody home?" Kitty giggled, waving a hand in front of my blank face. I blinked, and reflexively pushed her away.

"See these things?" Andrew explained patiently, showing me a curious contraption with two rollers, a few feet over from the line, which appeared to be controlled with a thin metal handle. "This is called a mangle. You feed the clothes through one end, and the rollers squeeze out most of the water so we can hang them up without dripping. I'll show you."

I watched in fascination as Kitty quickly rubbed all the dirt from a shirt, then handed it to Andrew, who wedged the collar between the rollers and began to turn the handle. As the rollers rotated, the shirt moved seemingly by itself forwards, and emerged at the other end significantly less wet.

"Neat, isn't it?" Andrew smiled, waiting for a reaction. "Makes staying at home whilst my brothers bring glory to England seem like the better option!"

He was joking, of course, and Kitty chuckled.

But just like that, I was back in Boundary. We'd had a contraption with two rotating rings like that, something that was designed to let one—and only one—of us into freedom. It was supposed to be Penny. I knew that, we'd all known that. Yet, somehow, I'd reached that machine first, and I'd been too scared to let her have the prize she'd deserved.

"Stop it!"

"Are you okay?" Andrew and Kitty asked in alarm at the

same time.

The mangle was nothing like the contraption in Boundary, but there was something about those two rotating rollers that brought back a flood of unwanted memories in terrifying clarity. This was precisely why I needed to let go, because until I did, I would never be able to belong to this world.

"I'm sorry," I said, taking a deep breath. "That...that wasn't you. That machine—the mangle—just reminded me of something."

They both nodded slowly, curiously. Eventually, after I managed to get my breathing back under control, Andrew mutely demonstrated how to use the pegs to secure the clothing on the line.

We worked quickly and somewhat efficiently after that. Like a well-oiled machine, Kitty quickly rinsed off the muck, passed on to Andrew who wrung out excess water using the mangle, who in turn gave it to me to peg on the line.

I was rather proud of our handiwork. By the time Julia arrived home from the town, the clothes had all been hung out straight, and thanks to vigorous wringing had nearly dried.

As we heard the car pull up, Kitty uttered the first words since my little slipup.

"You know, Evelyn, you've done so well, Aunt Jule might just promote you to head clothes washer."

"What?" I whined, sickened by the idea of redoing the whole awful process over again. "Really?"

"Yeah." She nodded wisely, and then added with a sly smile, "But I can 'elp you pull them all down again if you want."

I realized she was teasing and offered a forced laugh, but inside, I knew that I'd sell my soul to the devil without hesitation before I ever hung out the laundry again.

Chapter Four

Kitty's prediction nearly came true. Julia was thrilled with my work, saying that the garments had dried cleaner than they'd looked after she washed them.

"I had my doubts about you," she admitted, praising a shirt, which had been pressed perfectly with the mangle. "But you've done well. In fact, I might just have another job for a girl like you. We need to impress this surveyor who's coming, and I'm hoping to make a beef casserole for him, but I simply don't have enough time to make it myself. Apparently the twins are struggling in school, so the teacher gave me some extra homework I have to go over with them before Monday, plus one of our cows is pregnant and I need to have a look at her. Oh, and I must help Charlie fix the hole in the horse stalls too…"

"Don't worry about it." I smiled, trying to ignore the mounting panic beginning to build up again. I couldn't refuse to help, and, admittedly, I rather enjoyed the praise I received after doing tasks well. "Can…can Kitty help me, though?"

"Of course!" Julia seemed taken aback. "Have you much experience with cooking? I wouldn't want to pressure you into anything. I only thought your school must have an excellent domestic program, based on what you've done here…"

"If I have help, I should be fine." I tried to smile again, hoping it wouldn't result in a grimace. All I wanted was to sit down somewhere and doze off, but this place seemed to have no end of ridiculous chores waiting to be completed.

"You're an angel, thank you." Julia beamed, picking up a mountain of shopping bags she had put down on the ground.

"Need a hand with those, Mum?" Andrew called, appearing from inside having just disposed of the washing basin we'd used. "Any news?"

Julia passed him a paper bag full of boxes and cans, a line furrowing her brow. "Of your father? No, nothing. No one has heard anything, but that only means he's busy. He'll be home by Christmas, I'm sure."

We all went in. It seemed very dark inside, compared to the brilliant sunlight outside which reflected off the frost like a mirror in the fields. It took a while for my eyes to adjust, and when they did, I saw a sight that nearly made me scream again. Curled up in a ball by the fireplace, there were two enormous piles of black-and-white fluff. The creatures had protruding tongues, their eyes hidden under voluminous shaggy coats.

Andrew must have felt me freeze, for he gave a low whistle, and the two creatures came padding over obediently.

"Do you like dogs, Evelyn?" he asked, hand disappearing under the miles of fur. "These are Rosie and Tinkerbell."

"Those are *dogs*?" I found myself exclaiming.

"Old English Sheepdogs," Julia affirmed, and began to put away the contents of her shopping trip. "You're not allergic, are you?"

"No, no, not allergic," I mumbled, shuddering as one of them started to slobber on my feet. How foul. "But, um..."

"Here, try patting them like this." Andrew demonstrated.

"I...I'd rather not," I said, not making much effort to hide my disgust.

"My girls!" Kitty yelped, scooting around the corner and throwing her arms around one of their necks like an excited child. "Who missed their Aunt Kitty? Hmm? Who's gorgeous?"

I gagged as that slimy pink tongue licked her cheek, leaving behind a shimmering trail of saliva.

Andrew turned away, and I suspected he was covering a grin at my discomfort.

"Anna and Harriet?" Julia called, no sooner having finished one task moving on to another. "Can you come down here and help fix dinner?"

"Already?" Anna shouted back. A few seconds later she sauntered through the door with Harriet trailing behind. "It's so early, and you said we had to—"

"I don't care what I said then, I'm telling you this now," Julia ordered. "Mr Farrington must be impressed if we want to keep the funding, and I want you to use the beef I've put aside for a casserole, all right?"

"Yeah, yeah," came the reply.

"Right." Julia flashed Kitty and me a 'look-what-I-have-to-deal-with' expression before bustling out towards the horse paddock. "You know where the recipe is!"

A cool silence settled. Andrew excused himself, leaving us four girls standing alone, no one in any hurry to start the task. I kept my eyes firmly trained on the two dogs, not trusting them one bit.

"This is so unfair," Anna complained, finally moving over to the kitchen and beginning to rummage through the cupboards for ingredients. "Mum doesn't seem to realize that not everyone enjoys running themselves into the ground through chores like she does. We have schoolwork, and I'm exhausted from tending those blasted cows all day. James doesn't ever have to do anything, and he's only five years younger than us!"

We all watched her blabber, our expressions blank, no one volunteering to join in. Harriet moved silently to the pantry, but Kitty was still petting the dogs and I wasn't in any hurry to perform a task I'd never been required to do in the past.

"You two!" Anna summoned shrilly, turning to see us hovering about. "You came here to help, not observe!"

"Don't get your knickers in a twist," Kitty retorted, giving the dog one last pat before joining the glowering, younger girl. "Comin', Evelyn?"

"What do you want me to do?" I asked, having no idea where to start.

"Wash your hands," Harriet, who was closest to me, instructed softly. "The meat is in the larder. Perhaps you could go and fetch it for us?"

I thanked her, unnerved by her transition from crazy to calm. Perhaps Julia was right, and she had only been trying to scare me.

I returned with the meat as fast as I could. I still wasn't over the idea that meat came from animals, and being at a farm surrounded by them only drove that truth closer to home. Even now, it still made my stomach turn.

No one else noticed my disgust, as they were too busy doing their own jobs. It didn't take long for the vegetables to be peeled, chopped and thrown together into a pot with the meat. Harriet grabbed a tea towel and bending down slid the pot in the stove

A flame flared up inside and she screamed, dropping the dish so that it shattered, sending shards of pottery everywhere and the contents of our hard work sliding across the dirty wooden floor.

"Harriet!" Anna shrieked. "What was that for? Now we've wasted all the food, have nothing for the surveyor, and have this mess to clean up before Mum arrives and skins us!"

"I didn't mean to!" Harriet's blue eyes were wide with shock, hands still outstretched as if frozen. "It was the heat—"

"It's a bloody oven!" Anna hissed at her sister. "What did you expect?"

"No, no," Harriet said frantically. "The *Others* are attracted by heat, and I—"

Something changed in Anna's eyes. Her expression switched from anger to an emotion beyond that, a feeling that I couldn't quite place but of which I was glad I wasn't on the receiving end. Kitty and I watched from the sides, unsure of how to handle it.

"I told you," Anna said, as if the world contained nothing else but Harriet and her imaginary tormenters. "I told you to stop acting this way. There are no 'Others'. I don't know why you do this, but it isn't funny."

"They made me jump, that's all. I don't like it. I never meant to ruin anything, I was just scared."

"You know," Kitty interjected, her tone falsely cheerful, "we can probably still save this. It's such a waste to just throw it out. Here, I'll 'elp you clean everythin' up, then we can forget it ever 'appened. Want to grab a broom, someone?"

"No," Anna snapped, still glaring at her twin. "She can clear it up."

Anna gave a little huff and flounced out of the kitchen, in a manner that I might have once. Kitty flashed us an apologetic grimace and hurried after her, trying to calm her down, leaving Harriet and I alone with the mess.

I bent down on my knees and began scooping all the mess into a pile, deciding on sight that there were too many small pieces to save anything.

"They don't like Anna," Harriet whispered, making no move to help me. "They can hear what she says about them, and I'm scared they'll do bad things to her."

"I can't see anything," I said uncertainly.

"They're in the corner over there." Harriet nodded towards to where the fireplace was, and a chill crept down my spine. The dogs had moved to the opposite corner, and were growling softly at something I couldn't see. "They're watching you."

I opened my mouth to ask the next obvious question—what did they look like—but the front door burst open and Julia came hurrying in, face flushed from the cool night air.

"He should be here any minute so...oh my gosh, what happened?" she gasped, reeling at the sight of the dinner all over the floor.

"It was dropped," I explained, not sure if I should cover up for Harriet or not.

"Yes, I can see that." Julia ran a hand through her dense, curly hair, closing her eyes and rubbing her temples. "Oh, God. What a perfect disaster this is turning out to be." She flopped down upon the nearest chair and let out a huge, stressed sigh.

Kitty quietly came back downstairs and helped me scoop the

mess into the bin, pulling a face. "Are you all right, Aunt Jule?"

"I'm fine." Julia lifted her head and got to her feet. "I only hope we make a good impression on the surveyor. It will make a big difference to how much help we get from the government. Plus we just wasted the last of the meat and shattered my biggest pot..."

I got a cloth from the sink and wiped up the remainder of the gravy, wiping my hands on my already soiled dress. As I rose, the room started to spin slowly around me like a merry-go-round, faster and faster until I had to catch hold of the table so I wouldn't fall over. My head was fuzzy, my ears ringing, and I felt sicker than I had in days.

"Julia..." I gasped, swaying.

"Get some fresh air, honey," she said, in a voice that sounded like it was coming from far away. "I think I can see the surveyor's headlight, he's here already! Oh no, oh no..."

I stumbled blindly to the side door, blood pounding in my skull and breathing harsh.

What was wrong with me?

In the murky twilight, I saw the man get out from his car. Then I knew why I had suddenly become so sick. The man getting out of the car was Madon.

Chapter Five

Madon. Overseer of all that went on within Boundary. Keeper of order—usually through torture. Strong opponent to the idea of *any* of us escaping. And, to boot, the most powerful Ripper I'd ever had the misfortune to cross.

I covered my mouth to keep me from screaming. He wouldn't kill me now. He couldn't. Not with all these people who would know.

He seemed different. Standing there, surrounded by manure and run down outbuildings, he seemed more *human* than when he had in the moody backdrop of Boundary. There were deep bags under his eyes, and he was much thinner, so that his dark grey trench coat hung off his frame, several sizes too large. That being said, he was still the living image of 'sinister' and I was petrified.

"Madon," I whispered.

I must have spoken louder than I intended, for his head snapped around and for a moment, we stood staring at each other, suspended in time.

Run! I screamed at my legs, but they too were frozen.

Slowly, deliberately, with all the elegance of a cat stalking his prey, he began walking towards me. My breath fogged up the chill night air, my eyes widened in terror, my entire body shaking with a mixture of fear and cold.

"Evelyn?" Madon asked incredulously, raising an eyebrow. "Good Lord, you've really come down in the world, haven't you?"

I realized dried mud, gravy stains, and possible some squashed potato chunks, covered my dress and the wind had blown my hair wild.

"You're not going to say hello?" He frowned. "That's a shame. The real world has ruined your manners too."

I began repeatedly running my fingernail up and down the

31

bumps in the whitewash, up and down, up and down...

"I'm glad you decided to move on with life," he noted, glancing around at the silhouetted barns. "It was getting quite dull, watching you at that school, wallowing in self-pity and never getting farther than the town border. This isn't much, but at least it's a change in scenery. As an added bonus, your host family was very easily convinced that I was a surveyor."

Up and down, up and down, up and down.

"Stop shaking," he sighed in irritation, slowly coming closer. "It's not like I can hurt you anymore, and it's really quite annoying."

"You—you—can't?" I squeaked, heart thudding in my chest, hoping that Julia would come and interrupt.

"No." He sighed, suddenly seeming really quite weary. "It's not that it's impossible, but too many people would notice, and since everything went mad with Boundary, I'm not exactly favoured."

"People?"

"Yes. People." His eyes darkened. Then, like a flipped switch, the darkness vanished behind his new, odd, normality. "But done is done. I hadn't been expecting to back you to begin with, but—"

"Penny," I whispered, the name coming out choked as it caught in my throat. The memories were emerging from my subconscious, and I had to fight to hold them back. Memories of the trials, set to ensure only the strongest among us would escape Boundary and enter the real world. Penny had been the only one among us to figure out how to Rip, and combined with all the advantages that gave her, we'd assumed she was the obvious winner.

"Actually, no," he corrected with a twisted smile. "Penny was exactly the one I was trying to stop, given that she's the only one who could've freed the others from the outside. I needed to back whoever had the best chance of stopping her—Avery, I'd been assuming."

"Stop!" I shouted, panicking.

She's the only one who could've freed the others from the outside.

I hated this. I hated what my mistake had cost them.

"Don't be pathetic," he snapped, that characteristic temper flaring so that I almost found myself psyching up for punishment. "What, you've really tried to forget? You really don't want to remember?"

I bit my lip, blinking so that I wouldn't cry.

"I remember the torturing," I whispered to the ground, my fingernails digging into my hand. "I remember nearly choking to death in the fire. I remember burying Beatrix, I remember visions making my friends scream, and remember that moment when I realized I'd never see Fred again. It's *killing* me."

What was I doing? Something clicked inside me. To whom did I think I was talking? I had nearly forgotten, in my panic, what this man had done. I flicked a nervous glance as the parked car in the distance, and another at him, before gathering my courage and bolting as fast as I could towards the animal barns, where I knew I would find the others. Andrew had come outside, and I could usually find the older men tinkering around there.

"Evelyn! Damn it, this is important!" he shouted, angry now, but I was beyond reason.

I slipped and fell, adding more mud to my already stained clothing. My heart in my mouth, I jumped back up again and kept running as if my life depended on it; there was a good chance that it did.

"Andrew!" I screamed, skidding around the corner and searching for somebody, anybody. "Charlie, Pat, Gregory!"

I dug my heels into the ground and stopped. Harriet was standing right in front of me. Her face was blank again, but her eyes were red, as if she had been crying. I didn't know what she was doing, or how she got outside so fast, but I had never been more pleased to see another human being.

"Harriet, you have to help me," I begged, my head whipping around manically to try to see if Madon was following me. "Please! The surveyor, he's actually—"

"They're in the hayloft," she told me in that weird, distant tone.

I didn't wait for more details.

I followed her line of sight to the wooden, slightly rotten-looking building located parallel to the dairy barn.

Running without a corset was actually quite easy, and I found myself pounding on the shabby doors in what seemed like a matter of seconds. I was surprised that Madon hadn't caught up already, but it was probably a good sign that he wasn't willing to be seen around this area, with people. The doors opened easily, and I stumbled inside. The barn smelled of animals like the rest of the farm, the hayloft was filled to the brim with the dry bales, all stacked on the floor and upon higher ledges. A few pigeons cooed from the rafters, and I nearly ran back out again. Birds, like most everything else, scared me.

Stepping through the sea of hay, I steeled myself to try to make out shapes in what little light was filtering through the cracks in the roof.

"Hello?" I called softly, suddenly feeling very uneasy.

They're in the hayloft.

I horrible feeling crept up inside me at the word 'they'. Although she could have meant her siblings, intuition told me otherwise. What if Julia and Andrew were wrong? What if Harriet had tuned in to something no one else could see? And if that was the case, I was possibly trapped in a barn with a force more sinister than the one I was hiding from.

The barn became very quiet.

My mind was spinning. I had come to the farm to enter normal life, but if the past few hours were anything to go by, I wasn't in the right place. There was something haunting the farm that no one but Harriet could see, and whether it was

34

harmless or malevolent, it was too early to tell. I was confronted with ridiculously easy tasks that never turned out well, and now the nightmare of my childhood was back to torment me. I could feel the protective wall I had built around my emotions all those months ago start to crumble. Everything that I had refused to address for one year was rushing at me all at once in one huge tidal wave of emotion.

A hand roughly grabbed my shoulder

"Pull yourself together," Madon snarled, and my cries caught in my throat and I choked on them. "God, why did it have to be you, out of all of them? You got the prize, the future they were willing to die for, and all you can do is cry like a baby. Pathetic."

"You don't understand!" I shouted, past caring anymore. "I can't..."

"No, you're right," he replied coolly, disgusted. "I don't. But understand this—death is a chance you'll have to take, because if you don't listen to what I have to tell you, you're as good as dead anyway."

"There's something behind me," I sniffed, remembering Harriet's words. Paranoia was starting to set in.

He hesitated, and even in the growing darkness I could see the flicker of uncertainty cross his face. Then it was gone, and he retorted, "Be that as it may, what you can't see can't hurt you. For your own good, focus on what I have to tell you. Please."

Please?

He was pleading with me. Madon Farrington, murderer, overlord, supernatural menace, was pleading with me.

"Why?" I asked, my stomach dropping. "Why are you only talking to me now?"

"Do you remember D?"

D. How could I ever forget? Penny, favoured as she was, had started receiving letters from someone who appeared to be outside the Boundary, identifying themselves only as 'D'. At first the letters contained only words of encouragement. This encouragement became instructions on how to beat the trials, but as soon as Penny refused to sacrifice us in order to win, D became...well, violent.

"Of course," I whispered.

"We're not exactly friends anymore," he remarked dryly. "They weren't happy you got out instead of Penny, and if I hadn't interfered to make sure they wouldn't notice your progress, you wouldn't be here. They're coming for you, Evelyn."

I still had that overwhelming feeling that something was right behind me. Without meaning to, I began to move to the side.

"I shouldn't be talking to you."

"Don't be an idiot," he snapped, staying still as I backed up toward the door. "I couldn't care less about who you are, and I personally don't care much for your dismal attitude anyway. I came here because we need each other. Don't forget that I'm the reason you got out in the first place, and I—"

"What, you helped me escape?" I shouted, mortified to find tears pouring down my face. I was scared beyond reason, partly because of him, and partly because of the memories that had been stirred up. "When will you realize that I *didn't want to ever leave*?"

"When will you realize that what you wanted never mattered! Nothing mattered to me, except that Penny stayed where she wouldn't cause harm! I lost everything for that goal!"

I fell silent, reeling under the fury in his voice. I didn't want to relive these details, but something inside me longed to know the truth behind what had happened all that time ago. All my life, I still didn't know exactly what Boundary was, or why we had been trapped there.

"Why?" I whispered, my previous courage evaporating. "I'm sixteen now, nearly seventeen, and I feel as though I know less than I did when I was a child. My past makes no sense, and whenever I try to recall it...I don't know whether it's just nostalgia, or guilt. Guilt that I'm trying to forget my friends, when they might be trapped, and then there's Fred..."

Fred, the boy I loved, who lost his chance at freedom trying to save me. Fred, who convinced me to keep trying, even when the others had discounted me. I still doubted whether it was the right choice to leave him.

He waited impatiently for me to stop sobbing, pacing back and forth in the loose hay. "We have about two minutes before Julia Pearson snaps back into reality and starts to look for us. I can't explain now. I'll stay here as long as I can, but after that, you must promise me to stay away from them if they approach you."

"I don't even know who—"

"Their names are Demitra and Deio. You'll know them when you see them." He turned to leave and then added, "One more thing. It's clear you're not in the right mind-set to trust me now, but when you change your mind, use the Others to call me."

"Wait, the Others? What?" I was stunned.

"Tell Mrs Pearson I'll be back for Christmas." He sounded like the surveyor he was supposed to be, now. "Hopefully you'll be back to your senses by then."

With that, he left the barn. No Ripping now. No vanishing, no magic. Here, he was just as human as I was.

A few moments later, Julia came running in.

"There you are! Do you know what's going on?"

I shook my head numbly. "I haven't the slightest idea."

Chapter Six

As soon as I saw him, I knew I was dreaming. Fred. The fact that I managed to keep my head was also a clue as to the fantasy of the dream. He was sitting on the front steps of the manor, dressed in Victorian-era clothing, which was refreshingly familiar. He glanced up as I approached, offering me a warm smile.

"Fred!" I sobbed, throwing my arms around him in a hug and joining him on the steps. It was then I realized that I was wearing what had been my favourite lavender gown, with my hair long once again.

"Shhh, it's all right," he soothed, holding me tightly. "I haven't seen you in a while."

"You can say that again," I half laughed, half cried. "Oh, Fred, I've missed you."

"Have you, though?" He pulled away, studying my face. "You've tried to forget me. You haven't done anything to try to bring me back. They nearly gave up on you, Evelyn."

"I'm scared," I admitted, wiping my eyes and shifting around to take in the grounds. A heavy fog had obscured most of it from view, but I knew what was there; the rhododendron bushes at the manor's foot, the rolling lawns where we had played our games, the sunken graveyard, the eerie woods, which I had always disliked, nearly as much as Penny had loved them. As each image crept into my mind, the fog thinned, revealing more and more of the estate.

"See?" Fred squeezed my hand. "It's still there. You've still got it."

"I can't." I shook my head frantically. The fog crept back.

"Yes, you can. I always believed in you, Evelyn. The only thing holding you back is yourself. I'm not asking you to be fearless, no one can do that, but you do need to be strong. We're all backing you. We're still waiting for you."

I picked myself up off the steps, letting the soft material of my gown ripple over my fingers. How I had missed this life.

"Madon came to the house where I'm staying," I blurted. "Beatrix's son. I still can't believe that."

Fred said nothing, waiting for me to continue letting go of all the things I so desperately needed to tell someone.

"He said that D whoever they are...are after me. It seemed they wanted Penny to win. It's funny, imagine how much easier it would have been if everything had gone according to their plan?"

I trailed my finger over the rough bricks of the wall behind me, wanting to soak up as much of Boundary as I could, knowing that eventually I would have to wake up.

"Help me, Fred." I bit my lip, pivoting around. "I don't know what to do."

"Stop hiding, for one thing. Madon had that right. Pretending we don't exist isn't going to get anyone anywhere. You're a clever girl; you'll figure things out. Don't let people convince you otherwise."

I gulped through the lump in my throat, and nodded.

"Is everyone else here?" I asked, peering around. "Can we go inside?"

"Don't get ahead of yourself." He chuckled. "This is only a dream, after all."

I flopped back down again, cool woody breeze blowing my ringlets across my eyes. I had missed feeling like this, feeling like myself. The other me, with my short hair and scandalous clothing, was just unnatural.

"Can't I just stay here?" I asked desperately. "Does this have to be only a dream?"

"Does it matter?" Fred shrugged. "The facts still stand the same. We can't stay here forever."

I hesitated, and he pulled me into another hug, stroking my back as I buried my face into his shoulder.

"No more tears," he whispered into my ear. "I'll be seeing you again soon, all right?"

I sniffed, wiping my cheeks dry. "Do you really think I can do this?"

"Oh, Evelyn." He smiled sadly, holding me at arm's length. "I know you can. I never doubted you."

We sat there for a long moment more, surrounded by the thick fog and moist air, until somewhere far away, I was shaken awake.

"Rise an' shine," Kitty screeched in my ear.

I lay for a minute, trying to bring back the dream, but it was gone. The message, however, was there. I had squandered too long feeling sorry for myself and building a wall against my memories. Now, I was going to break down that wall, brick by brick, even if that took me another hundred years. Perhaps there wasn't anything I could do yet to free my friends, but I wasn't going to keep hiding. Eventually, hopefully, the answer would find me.

"Mind tellin' me what that was all about last night?" she asked, peering into the mirror in able to fluff her hair more efficiently. "Apparently Aunt Jule found you cryin' in the hay barn."

"It doesn't matter." I gritted my teeth, eyes straining against the bright morning light.

I never doubted you.

In return, I wouldn't give him any reason to. Madon had said it himself; he couldn't hurt me here. There was nothing to fear.

After a quick, cold bath to wash away the excess nostalgia, I pulled on my blouse and skirt, curled my hair, and went downstairs for breakfast again. Julia told me that I'd be helping Andrew and Kitty with the animals.

"You might want to put somethin' else on." Kitty observed my neat outfit. I saw she was wearing baggy trousers tucked over her shirt, and a part of me died. I had worn dresses for my entire childhood, and getting me into a skirt had been difficult enough—this was madness.

"I'll be fine," I tried to argue.

"Really, Evelyn, she's right," Julia put in. "You'll ruin that lovely skirt. I've got some upstairs you can borrow if you'd like."

That was how I found myself wearing both wellies *and* trousers as I prepared for a day of mucking about in horse stalls.

"Nice boots." Andrew winked, appearing in overalls and a sun-bleached shirt that set off the gold in his hair. "You look uncomfortable, though."

"It isn't decent!" I defended myself crossly, not in the best of moods. "Imagine if you had to embroider cushions in a dress, would you not feel terribly out of place?"

"Well, since you put it that way." He laughed. "Don't be too upset, though, the entire women's land army is probably living in dungarees. Times are changing."

"That doesn't mean I have to," I muttered, pulling on a jacket and trying to ignore Julia's hidden smile behind my back as she scolded James for putting too much butter on his toast ("Don't forget rationing!").

Outside, the morning was grey and silent. The frosted tips of grass peaked up timidly underfoot, the bare tree branches seeming like black cracks in the void. A crow cawed, breaking the silence, and I realized Andrew was beside me, staring, but not at the scenery.

"You seem absolutely mesmerized." He smiled when I jumped, but not in that half-mocking tone I had been used to.

"I've never seen anything like it." I shrugged, shifting on my feet. There had been something intense his eyes that I wasn't quite comfortable with. "The school was in the middle of the city, and Boundary didn't have any fields."

"Boundary?" Andrew frowned, and I realized my mistake.

Kitty saved me from explanation by galumphing in on us, kerchief tied around her ears and singing an awful song.

"Did I interrupt somethin'?" She raised an eyebrow.

"No," I said hastily, only making her smirk increase.

"Right." She winked. "I believe you."

"Not that she needs your approval." Andrew jostled her. "Come on then, let's go shovel some straw. You know you want to."

Kitty flashed us one last smug, knowing grin, then jogged

ahead.

The trousers felt awkward, as did the boots, but luckily Andrew could not walk very fast and I could easily keep pace with him. The ground crackled with each step, but even the frost couldn't mask the awful stench of manure as we approached the barns.

"This smell is really quite foul." I wrinkled my nose, sounding like my old self for once.

"Yeah," Kitty agreed, hands on hips as she surveyed the area. "The animals smell bad too."

I didn't see the joke until Andrew batted her over the head, at which point I laughed, embarrassed at the delayed response.

Andrew pushed open the doors to the horse stalls and limped inside. Kitty and I followed. But no sooner was I in, I was running back out again and gasping with panic.

Horses. I had never been in a small space with them before, and I hadn't realized just how *enormous* they were! Great, powerful legs stomping around in the straw, swaying heads thicker than I was, and I was supposed to be working *with* them?

"Evelyn?" Andrew came back out in alarm. "What on earth is the matter?"

"Don't make me work with those," I begged, pointing a trembling finger at the horses. "Please, Andrew, don't make me. I'll do anything else, absolutely anything, but those things are just an accident waiting to happen, and I wouldn't know where to start anyway. Please say that I don't—"

"Steady there." He raised a hand to stop my ramble, his face gentle. "You don't have to do anything you're not comfortable with. How about you bring us the fresh straw from the barn, and Kitty can help me do all the dirty work inside?"

"I'm sorry." My head fell forward, ashamed. "I don't know why the headmistress sent me here, when really I'm no help and afraid of everything."

"No, no, you're helping," he insisted. "It's strenuous work. I can barely do it myself at times."

I smiled shyly.

"Just use the pitchfork, load the bales into the wheelbarrow, and bring them over to us," he instructed clearly. "Got it?"

I nodded unconvincingly, but went over to the loft to give it my best shot. Horses...I shuddered at the thought.

The barn seemed friendlier in the daylight, for even the weak, clouded sunshine we had today made the grassy contents glow a soft bronze. The pigeons had flown away to do whatever birds spent their time doing, and it was oddly peaceful inside. The presence from the previous night had disappeared as well.

Self-consciously, I took hold of what resembled a giant fork, and testily prodded the straw with it. A rusty red wheelbarrow waited by the doorway, frost shimmering upon the peeling paint as if laughing at my weak attempts. After several stabs, I found I couldn't lift the bale. I gritted my teeth and tried again, determined not to mess this one simple chore up as I has all the others.

"We're ready for the fresh straw!" Kitty called from the stalls. "You doin' all right?"

"Fine!" I shouted back, blowing a sweaty strand of hair out of my eyes. If I was going to wear trousers, then I might as well go all the way.

I threw down the pitchfork and dragged down the straw bale, heaving it up and throwing it heavily into the wheelbarrow. Fragments stuck to my clothes and itched terribly, but I merely took a deep breath and dived right back in for more. I managed to lift a second one on and was ready to go.

Now I had to figure out how that worked. Push or pull?

I groaned in irritation. For the moment I had tried to lift the contraption, it had buckled over sideways and spewed the contents of my labour all over the ground.

You're a clever girl, you'll figure things out.

Would I, though? *Think, Evelyn, think.* The wheelbarrow

had one small wheel at the front, and two legs at the back for stability, right underneath the long, wide handles. This made it very steadfast when immobile, but wobbly when moving. All I had to do was find the balance. Well, that and patience. I at last managed it, though feeling embarrassed at the length of time it was taking.

"Not bad, not bad." Andrew wiped his dirty brow as I came stumbling in, arms straining to hold the weight of the wheelbarrow. He took it off me and my arms fell limply to my sides. I watched carefully as he opened the bale and dumped the contents into the stall of a horse, and observed how his muscular arms handled the pitchfork as he spread it evenly around. Kitty held the horse's bridle as he did this, cooing to it as if it were human, as she had with the dogs.

Then, Kitty handed the wheelbarrow back to me, and I went back to the barn to repeat the tedious process.

We worked like this for a couple of hours, until James came out to bring us a sandwich that Julia had made for us.

"Is this it?" Kitty wrinkled her nose. "What's in the sandwich, vomit?"

"Blackberry jam," James said anxiously, as if it were his reputation on the chopping block. "The last of it for now. Mummy said that because of the rationing, we have to use all the odd bits of food up."

"They're lovely." Andrew took a big bite just to prove it.

James beamed at his brother.

After the quick break, Kitty skipped off with Charlie, leaving only two of us to cover the remaining animals.

"You're doing chickens," Andrew told me. "I'll do pigs. Just sprinkle the feed around and collect the eggs."

I opened my mouth to protest, but he cut in, "Or are you too scared?"

"Of course not," I spluttered, but I didn't believe myself.

"Good. I'll see you when you're done." Chickens, it turned

out, were actually not that bad, as they did nothing more than flap about and never flew. They seemed just as confused and panicked as I was, perhaps it was the almost human intelligence I had seen in certain animal eyes that had scared me, that or a wildness lurking just behind a thin layer of trained control. The chickens' tiny eyes held nothing of these qualities, and I found myself laughing as they strutted around and bumped into the mesh fence in haste to get out of my way. Some of them even had pretty coloured feathers, and the clucking noises they made were quite funny.

The smell was awful, but I was used to it by now. I took a handful of the seed given to me and gently sprinkled it over the ground, laughing out loud as the chickens began pecking at it like clockwork toys. Inside the henhouse, the stench went from really bad to really *really* bad. I had to hold my breath and fumble around for the smooth, speckled eggs before withdrawing, inhaling some fresh air, and then diving back in again.

"Golly, that smells." I gagged, having finally taking the last egg. "There's poo everywhere! For such precise little creatures, I'd expect you to take better care of your personal hygiene!"

They clucked indignantly.

I glanced down at my outfit, smeared with muck, chicken excrement, and straw. "All right, perhaps that was a bit hypocritical of me. Friends?"

They clucked again, and I giggled to myself. I was sixteen, acting about eight, but that was beside the point; I had just completed a farm task involving animals without any error.

"See, Fred." I smiled, gathering my basket of eggs and stepping out of the coop, an action made much easier by my trousers. "You were right."

I handed the basket to Andrew proudly, feeling a flush of satisfaction at the surprise on his face that I had entered a pen of feathers and beaks without disaster.

Chapter Seven

After Madon's visit, two major things happened before October came to a close.

The first involved Andrew. I suppose part of me had been expecting it, but it had been that vain part I was trying to ignore. To cut a long story short, he'd confessed to have a 'crush' on me and wanted to know if I would go to the pictures with him. Girls at school had talked about the pictures or cinema but I'd never been and didn't quite know what it entailed. Then had come the even more awkward part of explaining my heart still belonged to someone else, someone who the world had decided didn't exist.

"Fred?" Andrew had scrunched up his nose as if recalling a particularly unpleasant memory. "Fred who?"

"Just Fred. No last name."

"Like you?"

"Yes." Why was I embarrassed?

Andrew laughed, a bitter laugh without humour. "You confuse me. I don't understand how someone like you could just appear out of nowhere, without any history, without knowledge of anything, and—"

"What do you mean, 'Someone like me'?" I asked, stung by something in his tone.

He insisted that he hadn't meant it as an insult. I stood out, he said, in a good way, and people like that usually didn't remain as invisible as I obviously had for the previous part of my life.

I wanted to correct him. I hadn't been invisible at all, I'd been living a much grander and fantastical life than most people ever would...but then I remembered turning around after crossing the Boundary and seeing nothing but trees. Invisible.

"You wouldn't believe me if I told you," I said when he asked where I came from.

"Try me." He folded his arms stubbornly, but his face was soft.

I opened my mouth, but the words wouldn't come out. "I can't."

"I understand. And I'm not just saying that." He exhaled through gritted teeth. "When people ask about my leg, I freeze up. I'm not sure if I could even tell you."

So we made a pact. It was my suggestion, echoing something Penny had done way back when. We promised that one day, we'd work up the confidence to tell our stories together, and when we did, the other would listen without judgement.

Even though I knew I could never return Andrew's feelings, I went about my work with a renewed happiness. There was something cosy about knowing somebody cared about me.

The week before Halloween the second incident happened.

"Mummy, can we carve a turnip?" James had asked as he scoffed down his breakfast. "Please?"

"Sorry, we can't waste food." Julia shook him off abruptly, clearly in one of her more depressed moods. Her face was buried in a newspaper, which she had been reading for the past hour in utter concentration.

James's face fell, but he didn't argue.

"We got a letter!" Charlie shouted, bursting through the front door, waving the envelope excitedly. "From the boys!"

Andrew reached out for it, but stood up so quickly that his stool fell back.

"Oh, no you don't." Julia swatted his hand away taking it herself. Out of the envelope she slipped out a thin letter, covered with scrawled handwriting. Her eyes scanned it for a moment before they dulled. She handed it to Andrew.

"Peter got into trouble for pranks," he summarized for the benefit of his siblings, who were crowded around him expectantly. "Robbie's kept him in order apart from that, though. They haven't completed their fighter pilot training yet. There's still a huge threat of bombs in London."

We all left for the fields in surprisingly good spirits, thanks to the letter and the absence of bad news. I abandoned the quiet, pensive group for the chicken coop, and began scattering the feed in a pattern that resembled the little dipper. Andrew had taken to teaching me about the stars in the evenings, which was quite fascinating. I'd taken to naming the chickens: *Ursa Minor, Cygnus, Sirius, Andromeda, Ursa Major, Cancer, Orion...*

I felt eyes on my back and froze.

"Please, don't stop on my account," someone from behind me said. "Do what you have to do."

I whipped around and took in the figure who had been leaning casually against the hen house.

He was of medium stature, well proportioned and handsome in classic sort of way. His hair was a light auburn, but his skin slightly tanned, so that the dark shadows under his heavy-lidded eyes didn't stand out so much. I felt as though I should have known him, and yet I didn't. A complete stranger.

"Who are you?" I managed to say, perplexed.

"Finish your chores, please." He nodded at the empty egg basket. "Then we can talk. I'm in no hurry, and these things should be done first—wouldn't want you getting into trouble because of me."

He was younger than I first assumed—my age, certainly no older.

Unnerved, I finished feeding the chickens and collected the eggs as quickly as I could, glad that the smell no longer made me gag. I knew I had heard that voice before—it was distinctive, yet I simply couldn't put my finger on it.

I stepped out of the mesh and faced him with as much confidence as I could muster.

"Would you like to sit down?" he offered politely, gesturing to a woodpile a few meters away.

"Who are you?" I repeated, wishing suddenly that Andrew was with me.

"I'm surprised you don't already know." He smiled, but

there was nothing malicious about the movement. "I'm Deio.
Deio Farthing."

Oh God.

The egg basket went crashing to the ground and the eggs
tumbled out splashing yolks all around my feet and wasting
about a dozen. Julia would kill me, but perhaps Deio would get
there first.

I couldn't believe it. This was D, one of those mysterious,
deadly forces in Boundary that had fought for power against
Madon and sneaked inside our minds at night, probing our
thoughts and altering our dreams. The D who had lead Penny
to near success, and who had caused Madon to flee after
that hadn't worked. How was it possible that such a vicious,
powerful, inhuman being, rivalling Madon, could also appear as
this pleasant young man standing in front of me?

"My sister sends her apologies," Deio was saying. "She
wanted to be here herself, but something came up and she had
to rush to Cardiff."

I swayed on my feet. Deio wasn't scary, not one bit, and
despite the withdrawn, guarded look in his eyes, I felt less scared
than perhaps I should have.

"You *are* Evelyn, aren't you?"

I nodded thickly.

"Do you remember me, at all?"

I shook my head. Madon had warned me that this would
happen, that they would track me down. But I could sense no
menace, no reason to be afraid.

"That's unfortunate." He sighed. "It would have been so
much easier. Madon has already spoken to you, has he not?"

"He told me you were angry I got out instead of Penny," I
explained, staring at the mess of eggs upon the ground. "That I
should stay away from you."

Deio rolled his eyes, which made him seem even younger. He
crouched down and began sifting through the mess of yolks and

shell, picking out the few eggs that could still be salvaged and plopping them back in my basket.

"So, do you believe him?" he asked, ice blue eyes serious.

I hesitated.

"Because he was right." Deio said it so easily, I had to think back to remember what he was affirming. "Demitra especially was...well, to put it lightly, beyond angry that you escaped. Mainly at Madon, but also at you. I think if I hadn't restrained her, she would have killed both of you on the spot."

I swallowed, eyes wide.

"I would like to think we've cooled off a bit since then," he said, almost apologetically. "Desperate times call for desperate measures. Yet, here I am, asking you to trust me."

"Who are you?" I repeated for the third time. "Really?"

Deio cocked his head to the side, evaluating my question thoughtfully. "That's indeed a tricky one. It doesn't really matter, as my offer doesn't change with my identity."

"Offer?"

Sensing he'd piqued my curiosity, he smiled even wider. "Yes. A little something to do with Boundary, and getting all your friends out."

"You can do that?" I gasped, stumbling backwards and nearly falling into the chicken coop. "How? Safely? What...what...no conditions?"

"Careful." He winced as I wobbled against the mesh fence. "Details are still being figured out, but if you help us then yes, it is possible."

Was it really possible for us all to be together again?

I was about to say yes, yes, and yes again, when Andrew came limping around the corner

"Evelyn, have you finished yet? Gregory needs help..." His voice trailed off as he took in Deio. "Who's this?"

"Deio Farthing." Deio offered a hand. "It's nice to meet you, Andrew."

Andrew's frown deepened at the sound of his name. He looked thoroughly unnerved. "How do you know my name? Have we met before?"

Deio grinned, showing a set of perfectly straight, white teeth. Then he turned back to me. "So, are you in?"

"Wait, what's going on?" Andrew jerked his head in my direction. "Evelyn?"

"It's really none of your business," Deio pointed out.

"I didn't ask for your opinion!" Andrew snapped. "And yes, I think what you're doing on my mother's farm is actually very much my business!"

Deio surveyed the speaker, something like recognition flashing behind his eyes, before he answered coolly, "Still living with your mother? As charming as that is, Evelyn and I are discussing something much more important, and it would be within your best interests to leave us alone."

Andrew flushed, fists clenching. I supposed that I should intervene, but what could I say? I was still trying to make sense of everything myself

"Is that a threat?" Andrew glared.

"Would you like to stick around and find out?" Deio said, a small smile betraying his enjoyment of the situation. "I would never intentionally hurt you, naturally, but—" Andrew's eyes widened as a peg in the coop fencing worked its way loose, and before he could react the metal had flown free and shot a just few inches from his face before falling back down again. "—accidents do happen," Deio finished, grinning.

"Get off our land," Andrew ordered, shaken. "Before I call the police."

I was reeling. Deio had just Ripped, here, in the real world.

"Call me sometime," Deio told me encouragingly, pressing a piece of paper into my hand as he shook it goodbye. "Nice meeting you both!"

We watched, dumbstruck, as he turned behind the woodshed.

"Wait!" I called, sprinting after his retreating figure.

Andrew's jaw dropped, but he made no move to stop me. "I'll do it." I took a deep breath, hardly believing the words myself. "But you'll need to give me some time. I can't just up and leave — there are many things I'll need to figure out first."

"Including your paranoid boyfriend?" Deio raised an eyebrow, watching as Andrew stood numbly around the corner.

"Yes. I mean no, he's not my boyfriend, but I do need to clear the air with him first."

"We'll wait," Deio agreed. "At some point though, we will need confirmation. You're either going to have to side with Madon or us, because we both need you and we'd both rather have you dead than working with the other party. Make no mistake, I'd prefer it didn't come to that, but there are things more important than a single life. Every day you wait is asking for disaster."

He gave a slight nod, turned again, and promptly disappeared into the back wall of the woodshed.

Dazed, I stumbled back to the coop.

"What the hell was all that about?" Andrew exploded straight away.

I shook my head and walked away. I didn't know the answer well enough myself to tell him.

Julia, as predicted, had a fit when she saw the smashed eggs. She had made every single one of us sit there and listen to a long-winded rant about how precious resources were nowadays, and how carelessness could mean the end of operations here, a decline in food for the population, and ultimately cause England to lose the war. In my opinion, it was a rather harsh picture for the loss of a dozen eggs, but then who was I to argue?

For the rest of the tedious day, I found myself performing quite badly at my chores. I could only put it down to one simple thing: Deio Farthing.

As empty as life seemed nowadays, I found myself confronted with an ultimatum bigger than the one Andrew had presented. The magnitude of what a harmless 'yes' or 'no' could result in was terrifying to behold, and was not a subject I would have willingly dwelled on were it not for the fact my life, and the lives of my friends, probably depended upon it.

As I helped Pat fix up a hole in the dog kennel, I mulled over the options. If I went with D, Madon would try to kill me, and if I went with Madon, D would try to kill me. If I waited too long, or did nothing, then I had about an equal shot at being murdered or not by the first party who grew too jumpy. The obvious choice was to keep my rather hastily given word to Deio and work with him and his sister to try to save my friends, if that indeed was their intention, and Madon had offered nothing but threats, and in the past he was never anything but evil and deceitful.

The only issue was it was too perfect. Too easy. Once upon a time, I would have hurled myself headfirst into a situation like that, but I had seen what the world was capable of now, and was much more wary.

To see Fred again. I could never live with myself, knowing I had passed that chance by.

So my mind was all but made up by the time I got ready for bed that night, mentally exhausted.

"Evelyn!" Kitty's grating voice smashed through my reverie as I pulled on my nightdress in the bathroom. "I think you should come 'ave a look at this!"

I splashed cold water onto my face to wake myself up, gathered my dirty day clothes, and padded reluctantly down the hall to see what all the fuss was about.

Kitty's eyes were wide with mischievous delight as she opened the door to let me into our room.

"Aunt Jule is goin' to have his head for spendin' money on this," she cackled gleefully, unable to contain her excitement. "But ain't it just the sweetest thing ever!"

For the second time that day, I was speechless with shock. For on my bed, were flowers. Red, round, and the size of a fist, dumped carelessly and without order so that petals had shaken loose from some of the blooms, and now spilled like blood over the counterpane. Rhododendrons—not even in season and which could only have got there by magical means.

"I don't think these are from Andrew," I managed to choke out, as Kitty bounced expectantly by my side.

"Well, who are they from, then?" she demanded. "Don't play stupid, we all know 'e has goggle-eyes for you."

I reached for the dainty little card tucked under one of the flowers, though I already had a good idea what it was going to say.

Do Not Be Fooled. M.

Hands shaking, I took one of the heavy blooms into my hands, knowing what they had been sent to symbolize. The same gesture had been made in Boundary to try to frighten us.

All flowers had meaning. For rhododendrons, that meaning was 'beware'.

Chapter Eight

"That was none of your business!" I shrieked at Andrew, tears of anger pouring down my face. "That wasn't your choice to make!"

"Look, I'm sorry, but if you're too blind to think straight, then—"

"*I'm* blind? Andrew, you have no idea what that meant to me! I can't believe you would do something like that behind my back!"

"Evelyn—"

"No! I'm fed up with people telling me I'm too stupid to make my own decisions!"

I slammed the door on my way out for good measure, sobbing uncontrollably. Locked in the safety of my room, I curled up into a ball on my bed, hugging my knees tightly into my chest and gasping for breath. My tears stopped faster than usual, replaced by a hollow emptiness that swallowed up all my other emotions in its vacuum.

I had made up my mind. I had decided, whilst accompanying Julia to town (not by choice; she had made me get into the car), that I would contact Deio and agree to help him.

I had placed the contact details on my dresser, in a place where I would not lose it. When I had gone to fetch them, however, I had found them to be missing. After further, and somewhat desperate, inquiry, Andrew had admitted to disposing of it.

"You have to see it from my point of view," he pleaded, obviously horrified by my explosive reaction. "A strange young man, who you claimed never to have met before, turns up and asks you to come away with him. Of course I'm going to be slightly jealous and irrational!"

Andrew begged for my understanding, but I closed my ears to him. I could only think about what this could mean.

Gone. That thin cord of hope, that little strand of possibility, had gone. Deio would assume I was chickening out, and that would be that. Gone. I'd spent too long wishing Boundary away, but after it had been waved in front of my face, I'd realized just how much I yearned for exactly that chance to set everything right. But it was gone.

"Evelyn!" Andrew called through the door. He was sorry, that much was clear, but I could tell that he didn't fully regret it. The apology was for hurting me, not for the action. "Please, open the door. Talk to me."

I didn't react. It felt odd, bearing this much sadness and not crying.

"Evelyn, please," he begged.

Over by the little shrunken window, the curtains were fluttering, as if touched by an invisible hand. Draught from the windows, Kitty had told me.

Footsteps announced Andrew's defeat, and I slowly uncurled myself, wincing as my sore limbs creaked with stiffness. My energy sapped.

Dinner felt even duller than usual. All they ever talked about was the war, the farm, the war, finance, Mrs Tibblet's plum jam, the war...

I supposed I'd better get used to it.

Resigned, I yanked my sorry self off the bed and trudged into the hallway. Harriet was standing there, frowning at something in the middle distance between the linen closet and me.

She had been behaving particularly oddly in the two days since Deio's visit, saying very little but acting as though she were processing a particularly perplexing puzzle, and concentrating only on that.

"Are you coming to dinner?" I asked out of politeness, my voice sounding flat even to my own ears.

"I'm too scared." She shook her head so violently for I moment I thought she was having a fit. Then I realized that she was simply trying to clear her head of whatever disturbing thoughts lurked there, and real or not, they were obviously quite vivid to her. "Evelyn, I'm scared something bad is going to happen."

Harriet's eyes were wide and frightened, but strangely sane.

"Is there anything we can do to stop it?"

"I don't know." She hesitated. "There's just a bad feeling in the air. I don't like it."

"Well, it's not like we can change anything." I pushed past her. "Not anymore."

I felt her eyes on my back all the way downstairs, along with a twinge of guilt at my abruptness. Still, I told myself, encouraging her delusions wouldn't help anyone, especially Harriet herself.

Without saying anything, I walked to the kitchen and began helping Julia set the table, and then placed the thin stew and bread in the centre of it so that it was easily accessible to everyone. The men came in right on time, quickly sitting down and arguing heatedly over how this war compared to the last.

"I tell you—" Pat leaned right over to whisper conspiratorially to Gregory— "this one is going to get nasty. Technology's grown so much better. London's going to be bombed into oblivion if they let their guard down for a single second. We'll win, of course. The question is at what cost?"

"Thank you, love." Charlie smiled at me as I set a bowl in front of him. "All these codes and whatnot are much too complicated for an old man. Stick to the farms, I think."

"The weapons have become utterly terrifying." Andrew sat down heavily beside me, choosing to ignore me as I shuffled my chair a few inches in the other direction. "I think they're working on something big, something new. They've got new weapons."

"Our boys, that's what!" Julia sniffed, setting out a small block of butter that was supposed to stretch around all of us.

"Peter, maybe." Charlie laughed. "I spoke to Ash Smyth the other day. Remember, he worked for intelligence?"

"Oh yes!" Anna sat down. "The very definition of tall, dark, and handsome! If only he were ten years younger."

Julia sighed disapprovingly, but it was too late. Kitty launched herself into the conversation with enough enthusiasm to make up for all those who had chosen to drop out at this point. Perhaps this was how Penny felt when Tressa and I used to have long-winded chats about such girlish frivolities.

"Mummy?" James piped up, eyes wide with a sudden thought. "Are we going to celebrate Bonfire Night this year? We didn't do apple bobbing on Halloween, so it's only fair."

"I'm afraid not." Julia massaged her temples tiredly. "Besides, what with the blackout, we can't have a fire."

"We have a fireplace." Charlie shrugged. "Maybe we could bake some potatoes and bob for apples in here? Wouldn't be quite the same, of course, but better than nothing. This house needs a little celebration."

"Please, oh please, oh please!" James clapped his hands in delight. "Please, Mummy!"

"Mum?" Harriet asked suddenly, face paled.

"Harriet, don't interrupt," Julia scolded, looking up from her conversation with Kitty. "Wait a moment."

"No, Mum..."

"You're being rude."

"Mum, listen to me!" Her voice rose to a panicked shout.

"Harriet, sit down," Andrew told her firmly. "Whatever you were about to say, can wait."

"No!" Harriet screamed, but I realized belatedly that her cry was not intended as defiance, but in fear. She jumped forward, arms outstretched, knocking over bowls and plates, reaching for something.

The light bulb exploded right above our heads, without warning. Glass flew everywhere and someone shouted in pain. Other lights flickered and died, plunging us into complete darkness. Chairs shot back as everyone tried to avoid the glass. James started crying, the dogs were barking, and Julia was yelling at everyone to be quiet so that she could think where the candles were. We moved around and I heard footsteps as Harriet ran away, and a slight protest from Anna as Kitty bumped into her.

My heart was beating fast as confusion swirled around me. Last time I had been in utter darkness like this was in Boundary, navigating through the ruins of the manor…

I felt something hard and solid behind me, my hands moving feverishly over its surface to determine where I was. Rough metal covered in a slight layer of grease, warm to the touch: the cooking range.

Something brushed past me and I shuddered.

"Matches!" Julia was shouting. "Get the matches!"

"Mummy!" James wailed, voice overpowering everyone else's. "It hurts!"

A person fumbled around in one of the dresser drawers, and finally struck a match lighting a candle. Light flared up from Gregory's hand drawing us to it like moths. In the dim, flickering orange light, the full extent of the damage was visible; glass covered the table and to everyone's consternation, the food. One or two of us had scratches.

"Damn it, Harriet!" Andrew wiped blood from his forehead, lighting another candle.

"It weren't 'er fault," Kitty chided, wincing as she picked a glittering shard of glass from the back of her hand.

"I don't think that bulb just exploded," Andrew snapped. "Harriet must have knocked it waving her arms about and fused the other lights. She's being hysterical…attention-seeking."

Julia surveyed the remnants of the bulb dubiously. I for one was certain that Harriet had not made contact with it at all. I was also sure she had not been seeking attention.

"Andrew's right." Anna stood beside her brother. "You can't keep letting her get away with acting like this, she could have hurt someone!"

"She went out the back door," Pat supplied reluctantly.

Some of us ran outside without waiting for more. It was creepy out there with the blackout, the moon hidden behind cloud and dogs barking like mad in their kennels, but I knew I had to be brave if I wanted to find Harriet first. I knew I had to, for if I could believe there was another world inside an invisible Boundary, then what was so insane about believing in mysterious, cunning forces that no one else could see. I was the only person around who understood what her situation must be like, and I hoped that I could discover what was fact or fiction — just in case a smashed light bulb was only the beginning.

Wind blew across the fields giving flight to wings I never knew I had as I ran towards the thin strip of trees acting as a hedgerow. Everyone else had gone to search the outbuildings, but if Harriet wanted to hide, she wouldn't have gone to those obvious places.

Where would I go if it were me? Besides the outbuildings, there was nowhere except the small coppice that split two fields. Sure enough as my eyes adjusted to the darkness, when I glanced down, there were footsteps imprinted in the mud, leading straight into the trees.

"Harriet, it's Evelyn," I whispered, seeing her hunched figure and not wanting to startle her into running away again. "Do you mind if I sit here with you?"

She had flinched at the sound of my voice, shuffling away from me, but when she spoke her tone was resigned. "All right."

Gingerly, trying to override my revulsion of the soft, mushy ground, I sat down beside her. Harriet hadn't been crying (I was slightly envious of her restraint), but had withdrawn into a sort of defensive silence that I myself recognized very well. At last, mulling over what to say in my head, I began to speak, but Harriet quickly cut over the top of me.

"Are you going to get the others, or not?" she asked sharply, her tone drenched in bitterness.

"No, of course not!" I replied, surprised.

"Then why are you here, to convince me to see the psychiatrist? That's all they ever do, you see. Switch between treating me like I'm actually crazy or just begging for attention."

Harriet stood abruptly as her voice rose an octave, fists clenched in anger. I stayed seated, unsure what else to do.

"I thought you might want to talk," I explained. "Sometimes it does wonders, knowing that another person understands."

"You *won't* understand, that's the problem!" she shouted, somewhat desperately. "I've tried talking!"

"Harriet, quieten down a bit," I cautioned. "They'll hear you. Listen...I know what you're going through. And I'm not just saying that. You see, *they* called *me* crazy too."

She stopped pacing, and lowered herself down beside me again. "Why? What happened?"

There was childish curiosity in the way she asked, issues forgotten for the moment. I watched as she sat cross-legged beside me, waiting wide-eyed for me to tell my story, but I was conflicted. I supposed if there was ever a person who might believe my tale then it was Harriet.

And so I told her everything. I told her about my early days in Boundary, before we had attempted escape, where Beatrix was our keeper and Madon was our controller, and the worst thing in our tiny world was the lessons. How we learned through books limited things about outside life, and how our thirst for knowledge about this mysterious realm soon outgrew the small confines of the library.

I told about happier times, the way we would spend hours playing in the gardens and woods, and I told her about darker times when we would be punished for breaking the rules.

I explained how we discovered Beatrix had powers too (made sense, come to think of it, now), and how Penny's obtaining of a key to a locked room had initiated the beginning of the end.

Harriet was shocked when I related how we had begun strong, united, until Tressa and Avery had split off on their own.

And when they had discovered something particular how it had led to Avery wounding Tressa, sealing her fate as permanent resident of Boundary, and propelling him forward to the end.

How in the meantime, for the rest of us, conditions had worsened as the estate collapsed around us. About how the legend, which was mostly fiction, had one reality and that was how many of us would be able to leave.

The fire, I barely managed to tell Harriet, during which Fred was lost, had nearly been the end for me. I explained how Lucas and Penny had found letters, and how they worked together to figure out puzzle after puzzle concerning them, relationship strained by the fact they were opponents in a very real game that would determine the rest of their lives.

Then how the end came, when Avery came back to us, and Fred had told me to get myself out. So I had. I'd pulled that lever, leaving everything and everyone behind as the world crumbled to ashes.

I told Harriet everything, everything except about D. Some part of my mind warned me that involving her in that charade would not be wise.

"...And so that's it," I wrapped up, throat sore from all the talking, and mentally shaken from recalling so much at once. "I don't know if my friends are all right, or what happened to Boundary after I left. I still don't know what Boundary even was, or how it could exist, and most importantly of all, I don't know if it is possible to somehow get my friends back out again. People here told me that it was impossible, and I'd been hallucinating."

Harriet swore in awe, struggling to find a word strong enough. "That...that's...I would never have been able to guess *that* had happened to you, not in a million years. And before you ask, yes, I believe you. How can I not?"

"Besides..." I smiled thinly, "...I'm not clever enough to invent a tale like that."

The release at telling my story felt wonderful and exposing

at the same time. It hadn't been easy, relaying those details, and I had skipped rather quickly over certain segments like the fire.

"I won't tell," Harriet vowed. "Gosh, it makes my own problems seem very silly."

I shivered. It had taken a while for me to finish, and now was very chilly indeed. There were shouts from the house, and I knew we didn't have much time before we were found.

"I don't really know how to explain it," she started slowly, brow furrowed as she searched for the right words. "What most people can't seem to believe is that I can't actually *see* anything. Whenever the Others are in a room, I just get this feeling, so strong I can pinpoint exactly where that are. Sometimes I can even feel emotion coming from them, like anger when you showed up, and sometimes resentment towards Anna. Back there, when they broke the light, it felt as though there were many of them in the room, and all of them had this menace. They've never done anything quite so obvious before, though. They make the curtains twitch without any wind, and they made me drop that casserole dish. It's as though they're getting stronger. It scares me, but like you said, there's nothing I can do about it."

I didn't know what to say.

"Only Andrew believes me." She sniffed, shivering too now. "The rest just tell me to shut up when I talk about it."

"Andrew?" I frowned. "But he acts as though he thinks—"

"Only in front of other people." She yawned, wrapping her arms tightly around her middle and getting once more to her feet. "But when we're alone, he likes to ask questions. Sometimes he gets really frustrated when I can't answer them, so I try to steer away from him."

The light and noise were getting closer, so I unsteadily got to my feet and tried to ignore the disgusting sogginess on my trousers from where I had sat.

"We should go now," I told her gently.

"They'll be angry at me." Harriet sighed. "But there's nothing

I can do if they won't believe me."

I nodded, and we drifted out of the trees. Harriet wasn't lying, that much I was certain of. The Others were real.

This reality was turning out to be just as strange as the one I'd left behind.

Chapter Nine

To James's—and Kitty's—disappointment, November fifth passed without so much as a candle being lit. Julia determined that supplies and time were too scarce to waste on such trivial things as festivities, and given that it was becoming more and more apparent that the war *wouldn't* be over by Christmas yet again, she felt celebrating anything was out of order.

But Kitty Rogers wasn't the type to let reality get in the way of a party. So despite everyone's sour mood, a few days later, I found myself being shaken awake at an ungodly hour of morning.

"Kitty...*what?*"

She held a finger to her lips, hair bedraggled and grin wide.

"I'm not dressed! Where are we going?" I hissed when she motioned for me to follow her out of the bedroom.

In answer, she tossed a coat at my head. "Trust me."

Then she was gone. I considered diving back under the covers, although by now I'd realized that there was no such thing as hiding from Kitty. Groaning, I pulled the coat over my nightclothes, yanked the curlers from my hair, and fumbled about for my thickest pair of socks before pattering onto the landing.

"Outside?" I gasped when she opened the exterior kitchen door, letting the freezing night air come gushing in. "Are you mad?"

"It'll be fun." Her grin widened.

Fun. I stared into the night, doubtful that anything out there could be preferable to my bed. Still, a part of me was desperate for even an illusion of fun after recent events...something to jerk the bad thoughts out of mind so that I'd be able to think.

I bit back a gasp at the biting wind outside, toes curling within my socks. Untainted by light, the sky above shone with an unreal amount of glittering stars, though even they were unable to break the swath of darkness that had swallowed the entire world. I could barely make out Kitty's silhouette mere yards away from me.

"Make sure you're quiet," she warned. "If you wake Aunt Jule, she'll flay both of us. Then I'll flay you again for ruinin' the party."

"Party?"

In answer, she reached out and grabbed my wrist, striding with such speed that I kept stumbling over every invisible pothole and pebble. At that moment, given one wish, it would've been a pair of shoes without question.

Out of the oblivion, an outbuilding loomed up in front of us. I recognized its peculiar squat shape as one of the equipment sheds—really, a glorified spare cupboard, as it held nothing but broken mechanical parts and other items that belonged nowhere else. Inside was a dank, musty smell that set me coughing. Seconds later, I saw we weren't alone.

"Hello, Evelyn," Andrew said tiredly, shadows under his eyes. "Kitty dragged you up too, eh?"

"Kicking and screaming." I yawned, almost too numb with cold and exhaustion to care about how dishevelled I was. At least the dark provided some cover.

Harriet and Anna were squashed together at the other end of the shed, Harriet looking half-asleep and Anna looking as though she might just throttle someone. They too were wearing pyjamas, so I relaxed.

"D'you think I should get James too?" Kitty asked. "Can't keep 'is mouth shut, but all the same..."

"Spare him this pain," Anna muttered.

Kitty hesitated. "Be back in a mo." Then she was gone again.

I sat on an upturned pail, squinting through the dimness to try to get some sense of Kitty's plan. She'd taken some of our homemade lamps—candle wax melted into saucers before being relit—and dotted them about on the dusty boxes. There were no windows in here, no cracks to leak light into the precious darkness outside, but as a result, the mustiness was almost suffocating.

Kitty returned with James, who seemed far too awake for our lifeless crowd. Anna buried her face in her arms and shut her eyes.

"Right." Andrew scooted over to allow James to sit beside him. "Tell us, Kit—what have you cooked up?"

"Well," she began, "I thought, since everyone's actin' so flippin' miserable lately, an' Bonfire Night ended up bein' nothin' but a typical day, we could have..." she turned around and brought something into the centre of our circle, "...a midnight feast! Like when we were kids! See, I got leftover pie an' biscuits an' toast an' I think some sausages that had somethin' green on 'em." Kitty poked the questionable sausage and shrugged, grinning ear-to-ear. "Ta-da!"

Silence.

"Kitty!" Anna raised her head, her mouth a tight line. "You've got to be *joking*."

"This is wonderful," I interjected. Anna redirected her irritation at me. "I think it's exactly what we need."

"I thought so!" She perked up. "Billy an' me used to do this all the time. 'Cept we'd usually have chocolate and sweets, but y'know, this is the best I could do."

"Perfect," I said, making a mental note to avoid the meat at all costs.

"Mum will kill you if she finds out you've been stealing food." Andrew reached for a biscuit and snapped it in half. It looked stale enough to break teeth. "And candles."

"Your gloomy faces would've killed me if I hadn't."

Kitty twisted around and fiddled with an object hidden behind an old wheel, and after an ear-splitting whine, music began warbling through the shed. I recognized the woman's low voice and quick beat of the song, surprising myself by deciding that I liked it—all the music we'd had in Boundary came from the piano. This was far more cheerful.

"C'mon." Kitty reached for James, who'd been poking the sausage dubiously. "Dance with me!"

Even Anna cracked a smile at the whirling chaos of their dancing. We collectively cringed whenever a foot or arm came too close to a lantern or piece of equipment, but strangely enough, Kitty wasn't as ungraceful a dancer as I might've expected. She followed no particular style, moving to the tune without a single care for what any of us thought. She looked…*free*.

"Anyone else going join us?" she asked after a while, face glistening. "Or are you all sissies?"

Nobody moved.

Well, I thought, *why not?*

"Harriet?" I extended a hand. "Partners in shame?"

Harriet blinked. "I can't dance."

"Neither can I. But I think Kitty's right—we need some cheering up."

I didn't have to elaborate. Harriet nodded, finally coming to life, going so far as to giggle at our ridiculous movements. Andrew clapped along to the beat, also laughing, and Kitty seized our hands so that we formed a single messy circle, spinning so quickly that the shed appeared to vanish around us. If only briefly, I found myself considering nothing but the moment.

"Anna!" Kitty cried, dragging her cousin upwards by her nightgown collar. "You too!"

"I don't even like this song." Anna tried tugging away in vain. "It's childish."

"Billy's twenty-one, an' he never had a problem with this kind o' stuff."

"Because he's *your* brother."

But Anna could no more resist Kitty's pull than the rest of us. The spinning grew faster and faster, much faster than the rhythm of the song, but we were all laughing too hard to hear the music anyway.

Eventually, the dizziness became too much and we collapsed down again. The air in the shed felt doubly suffocating, so in mutual agreement, we blew out all the lanterns and let in the night air.

"Weren't that fun?" Kitty asked happily, draping her arms over mine and Harriet's shoulders. "Weren't it a great idea?"

"*Wasn't*," corrected Anna.

"Yes," I spoke over her, quite honestly. "Yes, Kitty, it was."

* * *

In the end, none of us touched the food, so Kitty left to distribute it to the pigs before Julia noticed. The rest of us stumbled across the farmyard in silence, leaning in to each other for support against the uneven ground. A cloud had relinquished its hold on the moon, making it somewhat easier to see the house, but the short journey still seemed to take tenfold as long as it should have.

Anna cursed as she skidded on a frozen puddle. "Great, now I've gone and rolled my ankle."

"You should've done that on the way over," Andrew joked. "Spared yourself the dancing."

"Tell me about it. Times like this, I'm jealous of your leg, since you—" She caught herself and broke off. "Sorry, Andrew. I didn't mean it like that."

Andrew didn't reply.

"You're so mean, Anna," James supplied.

"I said I was sorry!"

"Yeah, but you still—"

"Can I have a minute?" Andrew interrupted, stopping. "I need to talk to Evelyn. Without you lot."

I stopped too, surprised. Anna, Harriet, and James frowned

at each other.

"Please."

Anna raised a dark eyebrow before continuing towards the house. The others followed at her heel, and just like that, Andrew and I were alone in the darkness.

"A car accident," he said, tone flat. "That's how I hurt my leg. I wasn't supposed to be out that night, but me and my girlfriend, Beth... Anyway, it was too dark out, and a car didn't see us, and we were both hit."

I digested this. "That's terrible. But...why keep it a secret at all? It wasn't your fault."

"No. It *was* my fault. I convinced her to break the rules. It's dangerously dark in the lanes at night, and I didn't care, and—" he exhaled sharply— "she died. And I didn't tell you because even now, I hate myself for it, and I didn't want you to hate me too."

"How could I hate you?" I managed to say. "If anyone was at fault, it was the driver."

He laughed. A different sort of laugh from the light-heartedness in the shed—this one contained no humour. "Maybe."

I searched for what to say, not succeeding. Words seemed awfully cheap in situations like these. So instead, I found his shoulder and laid a hand on it.

"Sorry." Andrew took a shaky breath. "I've ruined Kitty's mood."

"Gosh, don't you go apologizing."

"You've got no idea how much I have to apologize for." He sighed. "Look, Evelyn, I told you this tonight because I...I've got some questions that need answering. And I'm hoping you'll be willing to tell me your story in return for mine."

I hadn't forgotten our promise, so I'd been half expecting his request. After spilling everything to Harriet, the idea of dredging up Boundary again was less scary, though by no means comfortable. The Others enabled Harriet to understand the impossible—Andrew wasn't like that. Andrew, like the rest of his family, thought Harriet to be either mad or a liar, and I didn't want him to think of me as either.

But we'd made a deal.

So thankful again for the cover of night, I closed my eyes and rattled off my entire story as though reciting a rehearsed speech. Everything I'd told Harriet, from Madon to Fred, Ripping to D. When I finished, I steeled myself for his reaction.

"That's why Deio Farthing came to the farm," Andrew hissed.

"Yes," I said, taken-aback by his choice of question. "And Madon, too."

Andrew jerked his head. "So Harriet…her monsters are real?"

"It's all real. The magic and the monsters." When he didn't speak again, I added, "Harriet mentioned she thought you believed her."

I felt him stiffen, clearly surprised by this. "I guess there was always a part of me that wondered. It's not like believing in fairy tales and nightmares is encouraged at our age, but Harriet…she's so bloody convincing when she does her ghost act, I thought there must be some truth in it." He sighed, then forced a smile. "I owe her an apology, it seems."

He believes me too. I could have cried with relief.

"But then, why didn't you go with Deio? What are you going to do about your friends?"

I narrowed my eyes. "You threw out his contact details, remember?"

Andrew muttered something, too low for me to catch it. Then he began walking away from me towards the house, the irregular beat of his footsteps chewing up the night calm.

"Andrew?"

"We're going to find those Farthings," he said with an odd fierceness. "I'm not going to be the reason— I've made too many mistakes I can't fix to abandon the ones I can."

"Leave the farm?" I gasped. "But what about Julia? We can't!"

"We can. I'm a useless labourer anyway, and you…" He broke off, but I knew what he meant to say; I wasn't exactly their most valuable worker either.

The speed of his decision shocked me. The absurdness of my story, surely, should have taken longer than a heartbeat to sink in. I'd said how dangerous Demitra and Deio were, yet he was convincing *me* to chase after them? And leaving now, just when I was beginning to form a proper connection with Kitty and Harriet and the others—just when I was on the verge of *belonging* somewhere again—felt wrong.

But I knew I couldn't afford to think like that. The Pearsons would survive without me, and there was every chance my friends within Boundary wouldn't if I didn't intervene. I needed an ally like Andrew, someone firmly on my side and well versed in the oddities of reality.

Even if I did feel like I was sticking a knife in Julia's back by doing so. By stealing him.

"Okay," I said, once I'd jogged to catch up with him. "Let's do this."

Chapter Ten

We left the next morning without telling anyone. It was all very sudden. Just leaving like this felt terribly rude, considering how patient and accommodating the family had been, but Andrew had assured me there was no other way.

And so, without further ado, we left the Pearson household behind us, walking uncertainly forward into the pale morning light. For what seemed like forever, we walked in silence, the soft gravel crunching underfoot and crisp air flushing our faces a rosy pink. The crows, perching precariously on unstable fences, cawed at us as if taunting our guilt back into the open, until the bright sunlight forced them to fly back into the less offensive darkness of the tree line. The track snaked its way through about half a mile of farmland before finally joining the hedged main road, giving us plenty of time to contemplate the implications of our hurried choice.

"They'll hate me," I said, after ten minutes or so. "They'll think I made you run away with me. Maybe you should go back."

"Hate is a strong word, and I don't think they'd ever apply it to you," Andrew responded, fists tight around the strap of his haversack. "It's me they'll be most ticked off at when we return; I'm the one who's running away with a girl when I should be working as hard as possible to make up for not going to war."

"But that's no fault of yours!" I defended, surprised at the bitterness.

He did not reply, but fixed his eyes firmly upon the road ahead. We weren't running from work, I told myself. We were pushing towards something much more important than the meagre assistance we offered at the farm.

"So where exactly are we looking for these people?" he said eventually, craning for a glimpse of the main road, visible just ahead. "Do you remember the address Deio gave you?"

I shook my head sheepishly, admitting, "No. I didn't actually read it. But he did mention something about his sister going to Cardiff, wherever that is."

"Wales!" Andrew groaned. "I was hoping it would be a bit more local than that. Well...the nearest train station is about an hour away, so we better get moving if we want to make it to Cardiff by nightfall. It's a half-an-hour walk at the very least to the bus stop."

"How long is it to Wales? Gosh, it isn't more than an hour, is it? Because I couldn't stand anything longer than that."

"Uh, it will be longer than an hour, yes," Andrew said, turning his preoccupied gaze from the road to me with the barest trace of amusement. "But don't worry, think of it as an adventure. You've never been away, I suppose? Wales certainly is scenic."

The search was beginning to stretch out into a monotonous succession of task after task, and I did hate travelling about. Trains were all right, but after a while, I could see that even they might get tiresome.

"So, who exactly are these people, again?" he asked as we got to the main road, moving to stand on my other side so that I wasn't too close to oncoming traffic. "I probably should have asked this before agreeing to go on a road-trip to find them, but..."

I laughed hollowly, but the sound was lost in the choked engine of a car as it trundled past, filling the air with the stench of exhaust and petrol.

"The only time I ever spoke to them before Deio came to the farm was in my head. I don't even remember what they said, only I freaked out and woke up assuming it had all been a dream. Then Fred told me they had spoken to him too, just casually, but only once or twice. Penny, on the other hand, would talk to them all the time. We didn't know for certain, but Lucas was pretty good at guessing."

"And yet they were working against you?" Andrew wasn't humouring me; his tone was one of genuine curiosity and confusion.

"They wanted Penny to escape, not me," I affirmed. "There was a lot of tension between them and...and Madon."

I focused now on the narrow lane and not letting my feet slip into the ditch, half obscured by soggy grass and yet gurgling away with all the excess run-off from the recent frosts. Already, I was fed up with walking and ready to sit down, my arms aching from the weight of my suitcase, yet if Andrew's calculations were correct, we still had a long way to go. Between walking and buses, however, I decided that the former was the definite better of two evils, and would have gladly gone on foot all the way to the train station, perhaps even to Wales had that been possible.

After ten more minutes of trudging, my feet had begun to hurt. We were now on the main road. Even in my woolly coat, I was cold, and the cars were quite unnerving as they roared past without warning. I was about to complain, when up ahead, I saw the most wonderful sight of the day: a tall, outlandish red sign that clearly decreed 'BUS STOP' in bold letters.

"Look!" I squealed, pulling him alongside me so that we might be able to stop and rest a few seconds faster. It was even bathed in a bright spotlight of sun!

"Are you *excited* to go on a bus?"

"No. Only to defrost and regain the feeling in my feet."

I squeezed into the shaft of sunlight, revelling in glorious heat, weak as it was. However, by the time the bus arrived, I was dying to sit down again. Not only that, but waiting out in the open was worrying; what if Madon was to find us — or worse — Julia?

The bus that did arrive was chock full of people. I supposed there weren't very many buses running in the countryside, but as a result, it was filled to capacity with people scattered about thanks to the war. There were virtually no younger men around, at least none not in uniform, and Andrew got a fair share of curious glares. We stood for a good while, hanging onto overhead rails for dear life, until a woman noticed our plight and cleared her baggage off her bench so that we could squeeze in next to her. I closed my eyes, leant my head against his shoulder, and tried to ignoring the stench of tobacco, sickly lurching of the bus, and the wailing of a toddler being bounced on a lap in the row in front of us.

"If that child doesn't shut up, I'm going to have to kill it," the woman on my left snarled under her breath. "Or cut its tongue out."

I opened my eyes in alarm at the venom in her tone. Andrew laughed uneasily, despite her total absence of humour.

Then I looked again.

She wasn't a woman at all, but a girl in a shawl. Her strawberry blonde hair hung in dead-straight sheets, so different from the style of today. Her heavy-lidded eyes were grey and manic. The harder I stared, the more I couldn't shake their resemblance to Deio's.

Noticing me, the girl stiffened. "Maybe I should gouge out your eyes while I'm at it. Didn't anybody tell you that it's impolite to stare?"

Andrew was about to protest, when he realized what I was gawping at. He paled.

"You're Demitra Farthing?" I ventured.

She sighed. "Obviously."

That was it. I waited for her to say something else, then blurted, "How?"

"You were about to go on a wild goose chase to Wales, weren't you? And as amusing as that would have been, we just don't have the time."

"How did you know we'd be on the bus?" Andrew demanded.

Demitra sighed again, drawing her knees up onto the bench and tucking them under her chin. "I *know* things." As if noticing Andrew for the first time, she straightened up. "I didn't expect you to come along."

"Well I—"

"How are you liking this century, Evelyn?" she interrupted, her eyes boring into mine. "Isn't it just a blast?"

"I suppose," I answered uncomfortably, thinking of the dull clothing, freakish technology, and, of course, the war—not directly affecting me, but always there, a dark shadow in the background.

She frowned, studying me for a moment in a way that seemed to be both mocking and unsatisfied, before leaning into the window.

If it hadn't been for the screaming child and rattling engine, an extremely tense silence might have fallen. After a while, Andrew noted to nobody in particular that the next stop was ours.

"We're not taking the train," Demitra butted in, clearly more alert than she'd seemed.

"Where are we going, then?" Andrew frowned.

"Gloucester. I have a flat there."

"So we'll need a train," Andrew said, as though to a particularly stupid toddler. "This bus doesn't leave the county."

Demitra glared at him until he looked away. "I said we're not taking the train. I don't care if it takes ten years and a thousand buses, but I am not stepping foot on a train."

So that was that. I resigned myself to several more hours aboard buses, reeling from the presence of our new companion. Demitra may have been much more blunt than the likes of Madon and Deio, which I somewhat appreciated, but even I wasn't oblivious enough not to notice something extremely menacing lurking just below the surface.

Chapter Eleven

A bus had dropped us in one of the older, more ramshackle areas of Gloucester. The streets were cobbled, not paved, and the houses that edged them leaned in to one another as though vying for space. Soon buildings loomed up on either side, several stories tall, so alien compared to the sprawling countryside of the farm. The only vegetation around was the occasional roadside tree, or a tangle of ivy creeping up walls to devour brick faces. Andrew was taking it all in rather dubiously.

"I don't know if I like this," he muttered to me, fiddling with his haversack again. "It seems as though...as though..." He trailed off, shoving his hands into his pockets and glaring at the path.

I could see what he was trying to say. With all the windows gleaming in the filtered sunlight like glassy eyes, the shabby roofs blocking out the horizon, and streetlamps papered with week-old pamphlets crying out for readers to join the war effort, it was a bit oppressive.

"Oh." Demitra stopped so suddenly I nearly bumped into her. "I forgot to mention. *You* can't stay with us." A small finger appeared from under her shawl and pointed at Andrew.

"What? I can't leave Evelyn with... Why not?" he stuttered.

"Because I'm not a hotel, crippled boy," she said, with a sideways smirk at his bad leg. "However, the same can't be said for that building over there. Relatively cheap, so I've heard, but it'll do."

"I have no money." Andrew's face was growing paler by the second. "Not enough to last for very long, anyway."

"Not my problem."

I flinched at the callousness in her tone. Balling my fists, I said, "It is your problem. He's my friend, and I won't abandon him. If you think—"

"Oh, spare me." Demitra waved her hand dismissively. "Fine.

He can stay with us too. But first of all, you and I need a little tête-à-tête, so he'll have to occupy himself for a while."

Andrew glanced at me as though I was going to argue about this too, and seemed disappointed when I said nothing. As long as he wasn't being cast out altogether, I didn't see anything wrong with speaking to Demitra alone; there were some things he didn't—couldn't—understand, and I couldn't picture Demitra taking the time to explain everything to him too.

"I'll go...for a walk." Andrew sighed. "But if I don't hear anything in an hour..."

"Then you'll have to continue walking." Demitra tapped her heels together, impatient. "You don't make the rules here. I do."

"I'll be fine," I said, wishing I believed it.

Demitra watched him go with a smile. It wasn't a very nice smile, however, and half of me—no, more than half—considered running right after him. Perhaps this had all been a terrible, terrible mistake.

"Don't look so upset," Demitra told me, setting off again down a side street. "Don't you want to see your friends again?"

Of course I did. Her words brought the same shivers that Deio's had, and yet...did I trust her? The obvious answer was no.

It turned out that her flat was above a former fish and chip shop. We went into the main entrance of the shop, assaulted at once by the overwhelming stench of grease. A little bell tinkled innocently as the door swung shut.

"Miss Farthing?" A man popped his head up from behind the counter. He had a wet rag in his hands and an alarming amount of dust on his face. "Your brother just came in a few minutes ago. Oh, who's the friend?"

"This is Evelyn." Demitra smiled at me, this time a remarkably genuine one that people usually reserved for their best friends. "She's from London, so with the bombs and all... You don't mind, do you, Mr Hamilton?"

"Course not, love. You're not the type to bring in riff-raff." Mr Hamilton beamed, exposing rows of yellow teeth. "Do me a favour, and tell your brother he had someone looking for him the other day. I forgot to tell you."

"Did they leave a name?"

"Yeah. Farrington or something, it was."

Demitra's sickly sweet smile didn't falter. "Okay."

The second she turned her back to him, I watched it drop into a scowl.

To the back of the shop, a small door opened to reveal a steep staircase leading upwards into the flat. A musty smell overpowered the grease smell the higher we went, until I was gasping for air from this century. My arms ached from hauling my suitcase, which although small seemed to grow heavier and heavier. Finally, through another door at the top, we emerged into the flat.

I felt at once at home. Intricate, panelled wood covered every wall, stained a dark brown and covered with carvings. A fireplace containing still-smouldering wood stood at one side, opposite sash windows that looked out upon the street below, and, sandwiched between, bookcases containing volume upon volume of books and folders. The flat was void of decorative furniture and trinkets, with not a picture in sight; even the lamp, hanging from the beautifully moulded ceiling rose, was startlingly common. A shabby, rose-print settee and dilapidated occasional table were the only pieces. There was a small kitchen, almost too small to be functional, made up of a few slabs of wood over the top a couple of stained cabinets.

"Bedroom is over there," she gestured blandly to one side. "You'll have the settee. Andrew can...well, if he insists on staying, he can have the floor. We don't have a bathroom, so if you need to go, you'll have to go downstairs to the shop. No amenities, you see. Deio!"

I jumped as the familiar figure materialized from behind the fireplace.

"Evelyn." He offered a hand, which I pretended not to notice. "Nice to see you again. Unfortunately, I shall have to be a bad host and rush off again, but duty calls."

"Where?" Demitra frowned. "You know Madon was here a few days ago?"

"Brighton," Deio replied, and I saw immediate recognition flicker in his sister's face. "Shouldn't take long. And no, I didn't know that. Probably angry at been made a fool of again."

Their eyes both flickered to me, then back to each other.

"It isn't too hard," she muttered dryly. "Be careful, okay? Don't go closer to London than you have to, and be back in time to help me with you-know-what."

I was a bit taken-aback by the amount concern in her tone— genuine sibling concern.

"I will. And you be careful too." He turned and grabbed something from the behind the bookshelves. For a confused moment I thought I saw him slide a gun into a pocket. "Be civil. Enjoy your stay, Evelyn!"

I murmured something unintelligible, which only made them both smirk. With one last flourish as he pulled on a thin jacket, he was gone.

Demitra stood perfectly still for a moment, still frowning, then shrugged and sat down upon the settee before patting the area beside her as an afterthought. Dropping my suitcase, I obliged, ducking out of the way as she whipped off her shawl and dumped it almost on my lap.

"I suppose you want an explanation," she remarked dully, still staring out the door. "I can give you a limited one without breaking the rules, on the one condition you don't interrupt. What do you already know about Boundary, then, just so I don't repeat and waste time?"

"Um." I racked my brains. "Not much, to be honest. It was different, inside, people could do things that aren't possible out here—Madon could torture us at will, and disappear into thin air. Beatrix could use her powers for domestic chores. Penny could Rip too, move from one place to another, and you...you could speak in our minds."

Demitra finally wrenched her gaze from the door. I noticed her clothing beneath the shawl was surprisingly girlish and ordinary.

"Then there was the Boundary itself. It used to shock us if we touched it, but during the trials it only pulled us through to this kind of alternate place...towards the end, it was shrinking." My throat was dry, and the words were coming out very choppy

"Layers." She propped her feet on the table in front of us.

I stared, wondering if she was insane.

"The world is built in layers. In this layer, we're sitting in a flat over a chip shop, but in another layer this might be open fields. In one layer, there is the Boundary you know, but in this layer, it is simply woodland." Demitra spoke in monotone, as if reciting a speech she had presented many, many times. "Some practised people can manipulate these layers—some can even travel between them, or open spaces in gaps between layers or levels. You called these movements Rips."

I nodded slowly, not quite comprehending.

"Dear Lord," Demitra snapped, making me jump. She rose and walked to the window, then spun around. "Come over here. You look like a pre-schooler being briefed in quantum physics."

I blushed furiously, not knowing what she meant. Realizing it wasn't a compliment, I shuffled over to the window to her.

She unhooked a brooch from her dress exposing the sharp pin. "Pretend the glass represents a layer." Demitra frowned. "Got it?" she asked patronizingly.

I nodded again, but before I had time to question anything, there was a small Rip, and she had pushed the pin through the glass so that it went straight through to the other side without causing more than the tiniest crack.

"This is what it looks like when someone practised creates a Rip. No damage, very precise."

That made sense, at least. When Madon had used his powers, it had been so smooth and effortless, like a second nature.

I jumped as Demitra slammed her fist now against the glass, throwing all her strength behind it until spider-webbed tendrils began snaking over the fragile surface.

"This is what Penny is doing right now," she told me, continuing to pound the window. "Penny has great strength, but has no idea what she's doing at *all*. She's been trying to force Boundary open herself, but is only succeeding in creating damage like this."

I watched, transfixed, as the thin lines thickened and cracks spread to the corner of the window.

"There are things living in other levels. Fantastic, terrible things that we as humans cannot comprehend. As Penny weakens the barrier between the layers, they are slowly seeping through, and if we don't stop her, the barrier may be completely destroyed."

"Wait...*Penny* is doing this?" I frowned in surprise. "To the whole world?"

"Right now, it might just be affecting the West Country," Demitra admitted. "But watch how the cracks are spreading all over the window—before long, the damage will be spreading just as rapidly. There is only one barrier per layer and once it's gone, it's gone... This is why we tried to get Penny out before she started causing damage like this. If she was standing here instead of you, we wouldn't be in this situation, since none of you lot had this kind of strength."

The window finally lost its battle and shattered. We both leapt backwards to avoid the shower of shimmering glass, staring for a few heartbeats at the shards and splinters scattered across the hardwood floor.

So perhaps if Demitra and Deio's plan had worked, and

Penny had escaped Boundary, they would have prevented her from tampering with the barriers and we would have been stuck there forever. Now, because of Madon's success at foiling this plan, everyone needed rescuing.

"But...if we split Boundary...won't that create more damage?" I asked, trying desperately to comprehend.

"Remember the pin," Demitra reminded me, crouching down and letting the sparkling shards of glass run over her hands. "I know what I'm doing, and hopefully, you will too."

She stood up suddenly, wiping a trickle of blood onto her skirt from where glass had sliced her finger.

I watched numbly, cogs turning in my brain as I fought to understand. Demitra and Deio had figured out that only Penny was capable of such damage, so that was why they'd favoured her. Madon saw it differently; Penny had been powerful, and wouldn't have stopped until she'd freed us. Once she had escaped, that is. Now, somehow, the twins thought I would be able to help them stop her before all hell broke loose.

"You're mistaken," I stammered. "I can't help you. I want my friends back more than anything, but...we *tried* back in Boundary. I'm completely ordinary."

Demitra didn't seem worried by my admission. "Then tell me, why do you think you and the other five were in Boundary in the first place? Because you were all ordinary? Do you think Deio and I are risking our necks to interfere in the lives of six ordinaries? Do you think Madon killed his own mother to protect the interests of a group of ordinary children?"

I froze at the mention of Beatrix. "Protect us? She didn't—"

"Don't tell me what you think you know, Evelyn." Demitra stood up with such force that I flinched. "You don't know *anything*. You only know what we wanted you to, and that wasn't necessarily the truth."

"Then what is the truth?"

Demitra froze as if I'd reached out and grabbed her. For a

moment, she almost looked confused, then that sickly smile returned. "I have something to show you."

Chapter Twelve

The forest was larger than I remembered. After a bus ride, brief compared to yesterday, we lumbered down an overgrown miners' track into the woods I had tried so desperately to forget. Now, it was impossible. It seemed like only yesterday I had been running around in complete panic, having only just escaped Boundary.

The trees appeared enormous too, looming up all around us, branches whispering on a breeze as though complaining about our intrusion. We walked in silence, both handling the surroundings very differently. I had my coat pulled tightly around me, shrinking under the quiet disdain of the forest, whilst Demitra handled the challenge with an impervious arrogance, head held high and eyes focused firmly upon the track. Although it was my childhood home, I felt like a stranger here.

By the time a deer happened across our path, I was so tense that the sight of her startled me into an involuntary shriek, muffled behind gloves. The doe's head snapped upwards at my cry, ears flicking towards us and slender legs bent for retreat. For a moment, we stared at each other in frozen, mutual horror.

Demitra broke the connection her words dripping with scorn. "Haven't you ever seen a deer before?"

I watched the doe bound away, shaking my head. In pictures, of course, but never in person had I much experience with wild things.

Spotlights of dusky orange filtered through the canopy, as a weary sun spurted one last hour of light for our use. I could now recognize the abandoned mining pits, overgrown with shrubs now, but still prominent scars on the landscape.

"I'm going to keep walking until you tell me to stop," Demitra announced. "I want to see if you can remember exactly where the Boundary was."

I gulped. It all looked so different now, in a new season—plus before, I had been in far too much of a panic to take notice of where I was. Still, the gentle breeze seemed to whisper to me, sending me in the right direction, the leafless branches creaking like guiding arms...

After a while, I stopped. "Here. Right?"

Demitra said nothing, following me as I stepped off the road into the woods. Immersed in every detail, I navigated the steadily thickening carpet of ferns and trees

Then I saw it.

"Oh my..." I whispered, the blood draining from my face.

The creek. Barely more than a trickle, the clear water dribbled over a line of pebbles that broke through the grass for as far as the eye could see in both directions. In another world, in another 'layer', this was the marker for the Boundary itself.

"Remember yet?"

"Of course." I swallowed back tears. "Of course I remember."

"I haven't been back in a while either," Demitra remarked, almost conversationally, running her fingertips lightly over a bramble. "Quite the odd place, isn't it? Even on this side of the barrier."

"Like you can feel something else is here." I nodded, choking back another onslaught of tears.

"Would you like to see Boundary, Evelyn?"

"Is that possible?" I gasped. "Properly?"

She stopped pacing, her head tilting up towards a particularly large tree with sprawling branches drooping right down to about four feet from the ground, and a hollow large enough to fit a medium-sized person or child inside. The cedar. It was here too, as it was in the Boundary. A favourite hiding place.

"There are thousands of different worlds, layers, separated by thousands of barriers. We cannot see these worlds, and they cannot see us whilst the barriers are intact. Unless, of course, you have the right knowledge," Demitra explained, and I hung on to every word. "You need to know *exactly* what you are looking at."

"I do," I insisted, clearly seeing the manor in my mind.

"No, you don't. Or else you'd be seeing it right now. You have to know where it is, down to the last inch. You have to know what it looks like, down to the tiniest detail. You have to know *everything*, which is why we cannot see the other layers—and why we cannot see the things that are leaking through."

"But I do know it!" I repeated, whipping my head around, trying to find the telltale stone walls.

"Not precise enough," Demitra refuted firmly. "Besides, you can't even see past the trees that are here now."

Think, Evelyn, I told myself. Here was the cedar, the same as it was in Boundary...the question was, after months away, how detailed was my memory? "Surely, *you* know?" I said.

"Of course," she snapped, stung by my doubt. "I'm not helping, though, so don't even bother."

So, I decided to start small. I headed to where the land dipped into a clear depression, crouched down about two steps in, and closed my eyes.

Glittering black granite, shaped into a rough arch, smooth and cold to the touch with those awful words edged about a hand length down, *In Memory Of Beatrix Farrington*.

I opened my eyes. And there it was.

"I did it!" I crowed, delighted. The bottom of the gravestone was transparent; clearly, I was a bit foggy on those details. Right after the ecstasy, a wave of sadness hit, so strong I wobbled onto my knees.

"Impressive." Demitra bent down beside me. I could tell from the focus in her eyes that she could see it just as clearly, if not better than I could. "Try the house now."

Wiping my eyes again, I rose and went to the flattest, most solid piece of land in sight, and closed my eyes.

"Oh dear." Demitra smirked. "Looks like big things aren't so easy, are they?"

I chose to ignore her, taking another step forward and trying again. Nothing.

Every detail...rough, reddish-brown bricks that were slightly cool to the touch...ivy creeping up one side, right up to the wrought iron railing of the French balcony...the double doors, carved out of a thick, stained wood above a set of seven worn cobble stairs...

But every time I opened my eyes, certain that this time I had been accurate enough, I was rewarded only with the same tangled mess of forest.

"You're not in the right place," Demitra said eventually, impatient at my failed attempts. "For goodness sake—think about where you are. You lived here for fifteen years! Penny was quicker than this when I taught her to Rip."

"You taught—" I began, falling silent at the warning look she flashed. Jaw set, I scanned the ground for something, anything to give away my exact position.

Panic was rising. *Come on Evelyn, you're so close...*

Then I saw the rhododendron. It had no flowers left and only a few yellowed leaves, but I recognized it right away. Judging from the cedar, parts of Boundary were the same as this layer, which meant if this wasn't just a coincidence...

"Doors!" I gasped, surprised as the foggy, blurred image sprang up. About five feet around it was a wall, returning briskly to woods again where my memory slipped away. "Can we go in?"

"No."

"What? Why not?"

Her face set, she said, "Try sitting on the steps."

I tried, but ended up falling straight through as though they were made of nothing but air. The vision flickered.

"To actually touch something from another layer, you have to Rip completely into it," she explained. "At least, that's the way it works with Boundary. You can see the shadows, but that is all. Unfortunately, after the trials, the barriers between our worlds were sealed off, making it impossible to go back and forth."

As I stared, mesmerized and anguished, one of the doors vanished. Somebody had moved it, changed its position. Then I was overcome with a strange feeling, as though something had passed straight through me...

The thought of my friends—including Fred—being so close to me, yet not being able to see or talk to them, was torture. I understood what Demitra was trying to say, I understood what the stakes were, and I was absolutely petrified of the consequences. It was all my fault. If I had let anybody else win, they would have figured something out by now. I was an idiot then, and I certainly felt like an idiot now.

It was bittersweet, leaving Boundary. As I glanced behind me, I could almost hear a child laughing as she darted through the trees, taunting, teasing, 'You can't find me!'

"Bye, Penny," I bid the memory.

More silvery laugher, a strand of Tressa's flaxen hair blowing in the breeze, Lucas's tailcoat disappearing behind a bush.

I turned, biting my lip. So busied with walking away that I almost didn't notice Demitra glance back at something I couldn't see, face contorted with a something like sadness.

* * *

Faceless houses almost blocked out the overcast smoky sky, creating a dismal atmosphere, but Demitra seemed almost happy, sauntering along the street as if she owned the night. Andrew must've been panicking by now wondering where I was.

"Do you not get scared, living here alone?" I asked, wincing as I stepped into a deep puddle. "It seems awfully sinister."

"I'm not alone, not usually." She sniffed. "Don't forget Deio. Besides, there isn't much lurking around this town that's a threat to me. I've taken care of myself for as long as I can remember; me and Deio both."

"Is it lonely, just the two of you?" I pushed, overcome with curiosity.

"Nope." Demitra laughed with what appeared to be real humour. "I despise regular people, and being alone is the only way I stay somewhat sane. Yes, I can act the part, but inside I'm hating it. What's with all the questions?"

"I only asked two," I pointed out defensively. "I know nothing about you whatsoever, though I'm assuming you know more than I do about me."

"Reasonable assumption," she agreed, pulling up her shawl to cover her head. "I don't like questions, though. Penny was the same as you, except she did throw a rather amusing tantrum when we wound her up too much."

"You..." I bit my lip to hold back the tirade of questions I was dying to ask. "How old are you?"

She didn't hide her surprise at the inquiry, but clearly deemed it harmless enough to answer, "Seventeen."

Only a year older than I was. Odd. Deio, especially, seemed older.

"It's sad," I observed, half to myself. "You must have had to grow up quickly."

"Don't you dare feel sorry for us," Demitra snapped with alarming ferocity. "The last thing I want is your sympathy! If you knew—"

"I don't want to know," I interrupted quickly

Shadows emphasized every hollow in her face, showing the deep sleep-deprived smudges under her eyes—eyes that had clearly seen too much in so few years. I didn't doubt her guilt, but at that moment, I couldn't hate her for it either.

Nothing more was said as we turned down a narrow street of red-bricked terraces, our feet slapping the pavement.

"Demitra?"

"Evelyn?"

"I was—"

"Shut up. No more questions."

"Really!" I pivoted, hearing a sound from somewhere behind us. I thought I'd heard something earlier but wasn't sure. "I think something is following us."

Someone else's feet were pounding the path behind us, quicker, less rhythmic, as if it were multiple people who were trying to run without making much sound.

Demitra froze. Her hand moved under her shawl, her breath coming faster as the footsteps grew louder.

"Whatever you do," she instructed through clenched teeth, "keep out of it. It might be nothing, but if not, just let me handle it, all right?"

Eyes wide, backed against an alley wall, I managed to nod whilst biting back a squeak of nerves.

Three figures appeared through the falling mist.

I couldn't help but let out a sigh of relief. They were all women, so less intimidating; minds that could be understood and reasoned with I deduced. They could have been any age, all rail thin and dressed in rag-like clothes, and their hair greasy rattails. One was holding a knife in her fist, which was shaking with barely contained emotion.

"Farthing," the clear leader spat. "Where's your brother?"

"I feel I should know you." Demitra ignored the question. "But I don't remember. Enlighten me?"

The woman curled her lips back into a primal snarl, shifting agitatedly on her bare feet. I flattened myself harder against the wall, not so sure now if these feral creatures could be reasoned with. Demitra didn't seem too fazed, however, and that brought some strange comfort.

"Who's the doll?" The smaller one sneered in a scratchy voice that made me wince.

Demitra still wasn't listening, pretending to check off possible names on her fingers before shaking her head and saying, "Nope.

Sorry. Don't know you. Now, if you don't mind, I'm tired."

She tried to force her way past them, with me clinging nervously to her heels, but the leader quickly blocked her, waving the knife in her face. "No, not this time," she hissed. "You don't get to escape again."

I backed away again as Demitra snapped her fingers with sudden apparent realization. "You're Whatley's daughters, aren't you? I didn't recognize you without Joe—he's at war, I'm guessing? Heavens, Bella, you really let yourself go."

Bella's eyes narrowed, one arm outstretched to restrain a sister.

"Then you know why we're here."

"I do. And I think it's stupid, considering you've tried this twice already and it never ends well for you. Look, I've been nice, I let you live—"

"This isn't living!" Bella cried.

"Well, it isn't much else," Demitra wrinkled her nose as she surveyed their filthy appearance. "What I'm interested in is how you knew I'd be in Gloucester. Don't you lot live in London?"

"*He* told us," another sister replied reverently.

Demitra cursed, backing up so fast she nearly tripped over me.

"Evelyn," she whispered, eyes not moving from Bella's weapon. "Go back down the alley, and you'll find a general store. The sign says closed, but they're home, and they'll let you in. Wait there for me."

I didn't wait for more.

I ran so fast back down the alley that I skidded around the corner, all the while seething at my cowardice. Demitra would be fine I convinced myself; she didn't seem too worried. As for who had assisted Bella Whatley, it wasn't hard to guess: Madon, the only person who had ever successfully foiled the Farthing twins before and got away with it.

I was afraid of him.

Just as Demitra had described, when I rounded the street corner it was possible to see the darkened outline of the general store, lights all extinguished because of the blackout. Rain started to drizzle down as I ducked out of the shelter of overhanging shop roofs, causing my hands to fly to my hair, which I knew would frizz. After quickly checking for cars on the road, I took a deep breath and darted across.

A Rip shuddered through the night air, rippling from its source in the alleyway. A scream echoed, raising goose bumps on my arms, then everything went deathly silent.

Heart in my mouth, I wrenched my terrified gaze from that direction and pivoted towards the grocers...and found myself face-to-face with Madon himself, looking sinister in a hat and trench coat.

"Ah," he raised a finger as I opened my mouth to scream. "Shouting won't be necessary. Besides, nobody will hear."

"Demitra will," I choked.

He laughed coolly, remarking, "Already wrapped around her little finger, aren't you? But then, she always did have a way with persuading others her way was the only way. You're not the first to fall. I think, though, at the moment, she's too busy killing off my assassins to come to your aid."

"Assassins?" My jaw dropped at the connotation of the word.

"The Farthing twins have many enemies, all but few of whom don't have any power to extract revenge. It took minor persuading." Madon smirked at my open expression. "But really they were more of a distraction. No, I'm here to talk to you."

Weariness rapidly replaced my panic.

"Have we not already been over this? The surveyor visit, the rhododendrons..."

Madon didn't flinch as another Rip, sounding like a burst of static, followed by another high-pitched scream echoed from the alleyway.

"She can open Boundary and save my friends. Can you do

that?" I went on, finding courage from the memory of the recent visit. When he didn't answer, expression darkening, I pushed even further. "And if you want to know why I'm trusting her over you, I'll give you one word—punishments." I would never forget what Madon would do to punish us in Boundary.

He laughed with so much bitterness, the gesture was nearly a snarl. "Demitra and Deio don't usually lie, if they can help it, which is part of their allurement. But understand this—omitting the truth is just as dangerous, if not more."

He had a point, but it was one that I couldn't care less about. I knew they had committed all manner of atrocities, but they didn't affect me; I would comply until we freed my friends, and that would be the end of it.

"Why do you care? Why can't you leave me alone?"

Madon removed his hat, closing his eyes and pacing. "All right. All right. I can see you're still beyond reason. I'll let you be for now if you promise to push Demitra about your past. She's evasive because she has so much to hide. Secrets that will send you running back to me."

"That's impossible," I said with as much aggression as I could muster.

"So are you. When you change your mind, use the Others to—"

Like somebody had bashed a brick against my head, I was suddenly overwhelmed with dizziness, and something that felt like static.

Madon shouted in surprise, jumping backwards so that his trench coat billowed. I leapt out of the way, just in time to avoid being crushed as a lamp post crashed to the ground.

My head snapped up in shock, but Madon was gone.

"What...?"

Demitra came rushing around the corner of the alleyway, eyes wide.

"Damn!" she swore, observing the lamp post in amazement.

"Damn! Damn!"

"I didn't do anything."

"Of course you didn't, you idiot," she snapped, kicking the post in frustration. "I did! Damn it...I can't do anything anymore without breaking the bloody barrier! Madon is such a...such a..." She trailed off, too angry for words. Then, "This is what I mean." She pointed viciously at the lamp post. "This is what these things that are leaking through are doing!"

Still swearing, Demitra spun around and stormed off down the road, leaving me running in her wake. Mind spinning, I was certain I saw her wipe blood from her hands onto her shawl, blood that was almost definitely not her own.

Chapter Thirteen

"So you want me to find your parents?" Andrew repeated for the umpteenth time. "But you have no idea what their names were, where they were from, or anything?"

"That about sums it up," I admitted.

As I'd expected, he hadn't been pleased with how long I'd been gone yesterday. We'd found him pacing outside the chip shop, claiming to have been a minute away from calling the police for help in finding me. Demitra had only laughed in his face and waltzed off, leaving me to pacify him—which, eventually, I'd been able to do, after promising to never leave for such a long stretch of time again.

We were sitting having a breakfast of dry toast with tea in Demitra's flat. She had left on an 'errand'. Andrew thought it was more along the lines of body disposal, which I had to admit, was probably correct.

Andrew took a sip of tea, wrinkling his nose and pouring the rest down the drain. "I hate tea without milk," he complained. "What is England coming to these days? Oh, don't look at me like that, Evelyn! I'll try my best, promise."

"Good." I leant back, satisfied.

The room fell silent; there was not even a clock making any noise. My head was still buzzing, partially from lack of sleep, and partially from the emotional rollercoaster of the past few days. How odd it felt, to be sitting here casually drinking tea!

"I don't like Demitra," Andrew muttered into his empty mug, his face creasing into a frown. "Or Deio, for that matter. I mean, she must have done something pretty awful for those girls to come after her like that."

"Madon sent them," I pointed out, unsure why I felt the need to defend her. "And he would torture us for simply speaking out of turn, so killing someone for becoming antagonistic isn't so far-fetched."

Andrew raised a fair eyebrow, saying sarcastically, "That makes it all right then. Look, Evelyn, I worry—"

"Don't," I interrupted. "Don't worry about me."

Inside, of course, I was rather enjoying having him act so concernedly, though I would never admit this out loud.

"This is insane, you know," Andrew shook his head and got up to wash out the cups. "Sometimes, with all this banter about 'layers', evil overlords, and five lost teenagers, I can almost forget there's a war going on."

"Not a bad thing." I stared out of the window. Even in the weak, overcast light, I could make out the recruitment posters slapped onto every lamp post, and the obvious absence of young men on the streets.

"Isn't it?" He shrugged philosophically.

We sat together on the settee, thinking to ourselves, until voices from downstairs signalled Demitra's return.

Andrew made a face. "Great. Time to get thrown out with the scraps again."

"You can stay."

"Somehow," he sighed, "I don't think that's your decision. Besides, I can use this time—and this time, I really do mean an hour—to do some of your research."

Demitra scowled at him as he passed her. "What did Madon say to you?" she demanded. "Did he do anything?"

"Nothing new." I squirmed under her poisonous glare. "Honestly, he left as soon as the lamp post came down."

She cursed, kicking the kitchen cupboards and throwing down her shawl so harshly, a snapping sound whipped through the air.

"I hate him. I really do," she spat. "Damn, what was he *thinking*? He knew those girls wouldn't be able to do any damage, but arming them with *knives*? He wanted them to hurt me, not fatally, but enough to cause a scare, enough that I'd have to dispose of them. Do you know how *sick* that is? And knowing

I'd have to resort to Ripping, knowing what that would mean!"

She flopped down on the window seat. She had pulled her hair back into a simple ponytail, which was coming loose at the front, and her outfit was more era-appropriate with an embroidered blue blouse and grey skirt; not at all the monster Madon was trying to push me to think she was and nothing like the murderer who had killed three women last night. Only an average, if not slightly withdrawn, seventeen-year-old, possessing a temper.

"We need to figure this out," she whispered through her teeth. "Before it gets out of hand."

I waited — on edge after the outburst. I needed to trust her, I knew that. She was my only key to opening the door to my friends — but at what point would morals override that fact?

When people start dying? — a snide voice in my head questioned. That ship had sailed already; perhaps I was more hardened to such things than I believed.

"Sit down."

I did, immediately.

"Okay, then." Demitra took a long breath. "Let's get down to business. As you saw last night, Ripping is having an almost immediate effect now. Every time the barrier is breached, more Others are flooding in."

"Others," I repeated, frowning. "Like those Harriet saw."

For some reason, I had never made that connection before, and now that I had, I felt like an idiot.

"Harriet? Oh, that girl from the farm." Demitra's mouth curled into a humourless smile. "Yes. Some people are aware, shall we say, of their presence. Even I cannot sense them that well. All that I know is that most of them are attracted to heat sources, like fires, and they have an irritating habit of breaking things when there are too many in one area. Luckily, I'll be shocked if you can even *nearly* Rip by the end of today, let alone create something big enough for trouble. "

"I can't Rip, Demitra. Penny could, even Avery could a little, but when she showed me I never managed to do anything."

"You'll have to learn." She shrugged unsympathetically. "I need you. Deio and I won't be able to break the barrier alone. Not long enough to rescue everybody, anyway."

I gasped. "You mean there's a chance some of them will be left behind?"

"There's a chance the whole thing is so unstable, it will collapse on them when we try to break it." She turned to peer out of the window. "In which case, whoever's left inside will be squashed between the layers. But there's a lesser chance of that happening if you can help us, so I suggest you try hard. We'll need three to break the barrier."

She didn't care if anything happened to them. If Penny was the only one who escaped alive, the threat would be gone—but also her death would solve the problem. I swallowed, refusing to think of it.

"Tell me what to do," I whispered, glancing down at my nails and realizing I had chewed them down to the stubs.

Demitra smiled again, cloudy eyes shifting from the window to my face. "Don't worry. You'll be able to do it. I'd bet on it."

I grinned back. She was obviously more confident about that than I felt.

"That's why I was upset that Penny tried teaching you," she explained with a touch of bitterness. "The last thing I needed was for multiples of the same problem."

My smiled slipped away. Then why did she teach Penny in the first place, knowing the issues it would cause?

"Anyway—" Demitra clapped her hands, snapping those uneasy thoughts away— "I want you to levitate this teacup. Basically, you have to flex the space around it. I won't go into detail. Just concentrate on it until you can see the wobbly lines, then try to lift it. Simplest trick in the book. Also the best trick for parties."

I remembered my failed attempt to try to move powder pots

within Boundary and winced to myself. There was much more at stake this time around, however, and there was no bigger motivation than the thought of seeing Fred again.

I stared at the cup until my eyes burned and my vision swam, until I couldn't help but blink away the pain. Wobbly lines. What wobbly lines?

"I can't!" I complained, rubbing my eyes.

"Of course you can," she snapped. "Watch."

It took less than a heartbeat for the cup to rise smoothly off the table, before being set back down again.

"If there's any doubt, it will be impossible. Don't overthink it. Bring to mind another strong emotion to mask the uncertainty."

Emotional memories weren't exactly a rarity with me, so I sifted through each significant moment until I was nearly sobbing. Nothing worked, with every attempt ending in the same painful blink of defeat.

Demitra was rapidly losing patience, no matter how hard she tried to mask it. She clenched her fists and jaw, her foot tapping the floor until she could sit no longer and started pacing back and forth across the room.

"Again," she would retort every time I blinked.

"It's useless." I sat back in frustration, arms crossed. "I haven't even come close."

"You're just not trying hard enough!" Demitra shouted, the room starting to buzz with static pressure again. "You should be able to do this!"

"I can't do anything else!" I cried. "I'm not trying to be awkward, I just *can't do it*! Besides, what makes you so certain?"

She gritted her teeth, eyes closed in a struggle to maintain control. "Perhaps if I dragged Andrew in here and put a gun to his head, you'd be able to do it," she suggested coldly. "Freddie alone obviously isn't enough."

My mouth opened and closed, but no words came out.

"Except it isn't just Fred, is it," Demitra mused, words

sharpened to hurt. "Mustn't forget Lucas, Avery, Tressa, and Penny. It's their lives on the line too."

"Look," I said instead, my voice shaking a little. "If there is anything else that might help, anything at all—"

She cut me off with a vehement shaking of her head, causing more strands of hair to slip out of the ponytail.

"You need to be able to Rip, Evelyn," she hissed. "Or else the chance of this going badly multiplies by a thousand."

I wrapped an ebony curl around my finger, the tip of which began sporting a bluish tinge. I had to force back my tears.

I tried once more, but my eyes were so exhausted that they fluttered closed after a few seconds.

"I can't!"

"You have to want it more!" she screamed, something snapping. "Don't you understand? You're supposed to be able to do this, you're just not trying! Why do you have to be so pathetic?"

Pathetic. I hated that word.

Panic turned to anger, and as Demitra shrieked at me, I found myself wishing she would just disappear. Or calm down and just admit that I was ordinary.

Then the cup shattered. Shards exploded across the room causing me to jump back to avoid being hit.

"Did you do that?" Demitra asked, also having jumped back.

I shook my head, heart hammering. "No."

She stared as though she didn't believe me. "You must have. We're the only two people here."

I think we both reached the same conclusion at the same time. *Others*.

"You must have done something to bring them here," Demitra snapped. "What did you do?"

"I don't know!"

The lights exploded, showering even more glass everywhere. Then one by one, books began hurling themselves from the shelves, pages flying loose of their own accord. We ducked down.

"Stop! Whatever you did, you've got to make them stop!"

But how could I? I didn't understand what I'd done. *Stop, please just stop, stop, stop...*

Then they did. The rushing pressure stopped. The pages fell to the ground. And the noises faded. It went completely quiet.

My jaw dropped.

"Did you...did you actually stop them?" Demitra gasped softly, uncurling from her protective crouch on the ground and staring at me in begrudging amazement.

"I don't know," I muttered, flushing.

"Evelyn, Evelyn." She shook her head in disbelief. "You're such an unassuming dark horse, it's actually laughable. These things don't just pack up when anyone tells them to, you know."

"Is this good, then?"

Demitra bent, collecting all the papers up by hand—too nervous to Rip them together again. Her brow was furrowed in deep thought, and I bent down and scooped up the pottery fragments whilst waiting for an answer.

Eventually, she murmured, "Well, it's not what I was expecting. Better than nothing, to be sure, since you'll be able to help keep the Others under control when we split the barrier. And it'll buy more time. But it still means getting all five out safely is going to be a challenge."

I swallowed. "So...there's no chance I'll be able to...you know...do both?"

She shook her head stiffly.

I was proud of myself. Having special abilities was quite something to be proud of, even if it wasn't the exact gift Demitra had been hoping for. Maybe I wasn't quite so ordinary after all.

"Don't know how we're going to practise this." Demitra frowned, sliding the books back in place. "Not without risking serious damage. But imagine if you could use the Others as a weapon…if you could get them to do things for you…"

She gave me a rather disturbing smile.

"Excuse me. I have to go to see to something."

Just like that, Demitra had grabbed her shawl and was gone.

Chapter Fourteen

Andrew had booked into a cheap lodgings down the street not wanting to stay another night on the hard floor of the flat and with Demitra making him feel distinctively uncomfortable staying there. When we met up he told me that my news could have nothing on his. He suggested we should go to a place we could talk where nobody could overhear, that being the seaside.

"It seems a bit extravagant," I'd said.

"Trust me."

And that had been that. I had never been to the seaside before and was at once excited and fearful.

The train, compared to the bus, was heaven. I was beginning to appreciate them. Even in third class, there weren't many passengers except perhaps for city-dwellers escaping to family in the country; people were clearly feeling uncomfortable about holidaying during wartime. This meant we could stretch across a whole seat each, and I greedily took advantage of my own window.

If I forgot for one moment how fast we were going, and how many things could go wrong. It was actually one of the most enjoyable journeys I had ever been on. The train was smaller than most, and the windows opened about halfway down to let in a fresh breeze.

It stopped at a little station only a short time later, with only the two of us getting off. From there we walked in a silence that was not awkward, but suspenseful.

"Is the sea not dangerous?" I asked, my nerves starting to bother me with the increasingly salty air. "I mean, what if you fall in?"

Andrew took my hand in his, refuting, "No. It starts out quite shallow, and gets deeper very gradually. There are currents and drop-offs, of course, but as long as you stay on the beach you'll be fine. Have you really not even seen any large bodies of water before?"

"The creek." I shrugged.

The path wound up a gradual hill, gravelly underfoot and edged by patches of dead grass. It wasn't difficult to imagine how beautiful a place it would be in the summer, when the grass was bright green again and tipped with flowers instead of frost. A harsh wind blew overhead, tousling my hair into wilder curls and truly making me applaud my decision to bring a scarf.

"How much farther?" I asked through chattering teeth, panning the hill for trees that might provide a windbreak, but finding none.

"Only a few minutes more," he assured me.

I buried my face further into the scarf, skirt flapping around my knees so that it was difficult not to stumble.

"Hey." He stopped so that I bumped into him. "Have a look."

Cautiously, tired eyes braced for the cold wind, I popped my head up.

"Oh..." I gasped, my hand over my mouth.

In all my years, I had never seen anything so beautiful or ethereal. Ahead of us the land ended. Instead, pale, bare, rocky cliffs, many draped with rolling cloud, loomed nearly a hundred feet over the expanse of beach below. The sky was stormy grey overhead, but did not have the heaviness that often spoke of rain, and rather complemented the moody setting quite perfectly. Below us lay a bay, a half-moon mixture of pebbles and sand, untouched by people in the protective cradle of cliff and cloud. Then there was the sea, another beast entirely. The broken surface was the colour of steel, lapping the shoreline hungrily and writhing under a breeze that whipped wildly over its flat back. This couldn't all be water, not all of it! In every direction, all the way to the misty horizon, the sea marked its domain.

A steep path snaked downwards just in front of us, zigzagging quite precariously.

"Need a hand?" Andrew offered, edging down a few feet in

front of me.

"No, I can do it, thanks." I took a brave step by myself, still transfixed by the hypnotic crashing of waves on the shore.

A second later, I was on my rear, having missed my footing entirely and skidded right down a substantial portion of the path. Embarrassed and blushing a furious red, I shook the gravel from my clothes and took Andrew's extended hand.

"No shame in accepting a gentleman's gallantry," he chuckled, winking. "Actually, you have no idea how many times I've ended up on my backside trying to scale these cliffs."

"You come here often?" I inquired, tongue peeking out in concentration.

"Well, we used to." His face fell. It was then I realized how difficult it must be for Andrew to be walking down this steep path. I had grown so accustomed to his limp now that it was easy to forget the mobility issues he was struggling with every breathing moment. Even now, supporting me in the crook of his arm, pain bubbled just below the surface contorting his face.

I unhooked my arm, using the rocks instead to steady myself.

"I was fine!"

"No shame," I repeated gently.

It was a relief to be finally on flat ground. I leaned against the cliff-face to catch my breath, observing the scene in enamoured wonder. Now, only a few leaps away, the true power of the sea was evident. Waves slapped the sand before grudgingly withdrawing back into the body, pounding the ancient rock formations without mercy.

Andrew kicked off his shoes, nodding for me to follow suit. I wrinkled my nose, but curiosity overpowered propriety as I wondered what sand might feel like underfoot. The answer turned out to be delightfully soft and only a little damp, oozing between my toes as I ran after him.

"What are you doing?" I called, grumbling as the wind whipped my hair in front of my eyes. "Andrew!"

He grabbed my hand, tugging me towards the crashing waves. I protested half-heartedly, body tensed against an unknown element.

Then water was spraying all over me, cold and salty. I shrieked in surprise, eyes flying open, wrenching away back towards solid land.

"It's not going to hurt you," Andrew promised, eyes laughing. "Trust me."

I bit my lip, staring out towards the endless sea and imagining what it would be like to submerge myself completely in the water. Not like a bath, of course and I was wary that there was much more chance of drowning. "I do trust you."

I took a determined step forwards, shuddering as my feet disappeared underneath the foamy water. It was cold, much too cold, but fantastic.

"It's like something from a fairy tale," I exclaimed, turning towards Andrew with bright eyes. "I can't believe it's real!"

"Compared to Boundary, this is hardly a fantasy."

"Perhaps not to you. But it is to me."

I inhaled deeply, suddenly not noticing the bracing wind yanking at my hair, or the sea spray soaking my clothes, or the darkening clouds overhead. It was a world of its own down here, a place where nothing could touch me.

Andrew was in knee-deep, trousers rolled up. I wasn't planning to go in that that far, but I did shuffle a little bit farther so that my ankles went under. It was more pebbly and less sandy here, but the numbing cold masked any discomfort this may have caused.

Then I slipped. With a gasp, my feet skidded on the pebbles and launched me into the water.

"Evelyn!" Andrew gasped, splashing over as fast as he could.

"I-I'm f-f-f-fine," I chattered. Everything was soaked, including my hair! "J-just s-s-seem to b-be f-f-falling over a lot t-t-today."

"I've a blanket in my haversack," he remembered, limping as fast as he could towards the path, where he'd left the bag.

My only outfit was ruined, hanging off my frame in a sorry sail of heavy fabric. I was shivering uncontrollably and I'd twisted my ankle and it was throbbing. Slowly, I lowered myself down sighing with tight release as the icy water washed over me, numbing everything.

That was when I abandoned myself, and let my head fall back into the water so that my raven hair floated around my face. Reality was plunged into a frigid blur as I lay back, the rolling picture of clouds above now directly in my vision.

"Evelyn?" Andrew shouted from farther up the beach. "What are you doing? You're going to freeze to death!"

His concerned but angry voice jerked me to my senses. I dragged myself to my feet and padded over to the shore. He shook his head in disbelief, handing me the blanket and muttering about how idiotic I could be. I must've looked a fright with my makeup washed off, and my curls dragged down with water into messy rattails.

"I was saving this to sit on." He gestured to the blanket. "But I suppose we'll have to make do with the sand."

I nodded, peeling off my soaked coat and sitting down. Andrew wrapped the blanket around me. He rubbed me with it bringing some feeling back into my numbed limbs. My nerves were buzzing, and despite the fact I was practically an icicle, I felt alive.

"So, now you've fully experienced the glory of the sea, want to exchange information?" He sat down beside me. "I'm actually quite chuffed about how much I've found."

"Definitely."

"You first."

"Well…I think I might be able to influence the Others," I said. "Those things Harriet can see."

Andrew blinked. "Right. What?"

So I recounted a rather summarized version of what Demitra had told me about the layers. I could tell before I was finished he didn't quite believe it, but I knew just as certainly he wouldn't challenge it.

"That's good," he said eventually, perhaps not trusting himself to think further into it. "Well, I...I think I found your parents."

"You what?" I gasped, shocked, wrenching free of the blanket to face him. "How? We had nothing to go on."

"The librarian I spoke to remembered something she had recorded in the newspaper archives," Andrew explained, buoyed by my enthusiasm. "It might just be coincidence, but then again, it might not."

I glanced at the sea in wonder. Was it foolish to hope? That after all this time, I might still have a proper family waiting for me, one like the Pearson's? Would they remember me? Why had I been taken from them in the first place? Had they given up trying to find me?

Andrew produced a crumpled stack of notes from his haversack, but thanks to the vigorous wind, it was nearly impossible to hold on to them.

"Just tell me what it says," I suggested, bundling back down inside my blanket. "I could never steady my hands enough anyway."

"All right," he agreed. "But, Evelyn, it isn't good news."

"Tell me," I instructed, throat tightening.

"Lucas Redding, Fred Ashton, Avery Sadler, Tressa McGinley, and Evelyn Stuart. Five children between the ages of two weeks to eighteen months old, all reported missing within the same space of about a month. None of them were ever found, so the incident was covered up by the police. But what linked them together were the families: all found dead. Every member of the family would be found as if they had just had an accident: tripping down the stairs with a knife in hand, banging their head on a kitchen sink, unintentional overdose on prescription drugs. In fact, each death would have seemed like an accident, were it not for the fact the entire family was dead, and the infants were missing."

The knot, which had been growing steadily in my stomach, moved to my throat, and I uttered a small cry. I was Evelyn Stuart, and my family was dead. Murdered.

"I'm sorry." Andrew awkwardly put his arm around me. "But, if it's not insensitive, at least you know who you are now."

"Why? Who would...who would do such a thing? How did we end up in Boundary? It just creates more questions."

The sea spray mixed with my silent tears; grief for a life I would now never know. The euphoria had worn off, and it was as if a little shimmer of hope inside me had died.

"Was there no mention of Penny?" I mumbled into the blanket.

"No. Only you five."

Odd. It was a shame, now the five of us would have last names; she'd be jealous when we were together again.

Then I saw a glimmer of coins from Andrew's bag. Nothing much, of course, only a handful of pennies and... "Oh my gosh," I gasped suddenly, realization hitting me like a sharp slap in the face. "How could I not have noticed it before?"

Before Andrew could ask what the issue was, I had jumped straight up so that the blanket heaped onto the sand.

"Penny Farthing!" I exclaimed, laughing and crying at the same time. "I bet they thought it was hilarious, didn't they?"

"Isn't that a type of old bicycle?" Andrew hadn't quite caught on.

"Demitra and Deio *Farthing*." I tossed two coins at him, a penny, and a farthing. "If they...if they named her... Penny was always more powerful than us, wasn't she? D always favoured her, even though technically any of us could have caused damage. Even in appearance—how could it have taken me this long? Penny *Farthing*."

Andrew's mouth was open, his face paled.

"Are you sure?" he asked, voice wavering.

"Of course not," I said, excitedly. "But wouldn't it make sense?"

"Still, if that were the case, why would Penny be inside Boundary while the other two ran around outside?" Andrew argued hotly.

I shrugged. "I'll have to ask Demitra. I might be wrong, but if the twins are using aliases, they probably just assumed nobody would make the connection... It was a joke..."

I realized I was babbling, and abruptly shut my mouth.

Evelyn Stuart. It sounded strange—much too long. Miss Stuart, they would call me now. Very proper.

"We should go," Andrew suggested, beginning to pack away the notes. "Before you catch a cold. I'll try to look into it a bit more, now we have names to go by."

"Yes."

I helped to pack the blanket away, and wiped the sand off my soggy skirt. Then, after a final goodbye to the sea, we started the precarious trek up the path again.

Chapter Fifteen

Three days, that was how long it took me to pluck up enough courage to confront Demitra. Three days of awkward silence, with me left alone to stew over the results of Andrew's discovery.

I cracked during lunchtime. We were sitting at the dining table. Demitra had come back late over the past few nights, and without a touch of makeup, hair waving slightly owing to the absence of brushing, she seemed to be as unintimidating as were possible—for her, at least.

"Demitra?" I cleared my throat. Why was I so nervous? I was totally within my rights to ask questions, wasn't I?

"Mm?" She didn't look up from her novel.

"Would it be possible to ask you about a few things?"

"Depends." Still scanning the book page, she didn't look up.

"You see...Andrew has being doing some research about our past, and he found some very interesting—odd really— information."

Finally, she took the bait. Her head jerked upright so fast, it was a miracle her neck didn't snap. I kept my face a demure, innocently curious mask, hoping she couldn't see the anxiety hidden there.

"What did the paper say?" Demitra inquired tightly, pushing the book away with the tips of her fingers and picking up a glass of water. Odd as it was, she seemed more anxious than I was.

I paused, trying to summarize it all in my head before speaking. Eventually, I decided to cut to the chase and get the most nagging part over with first. "Is Penny your sister?"

The reaction was immediate and not at all what I had expected. Demitra's expression was neutral for a moment, but when the emotion returned it wasn't rage or even shock, but relief.

"It took you a while, didn't it?" She smirked, leaning back in her chair. "I thought the naming part was funny."

"Funny?" I uttered incredulously. "Did you ever tell Penny?"

"Of course not. Heck, she still thinks D is some monster, not her two older siblings."

Demitra took a sip of water, smiling secretly to herself. I took a steadying breath and pushed on.

"Then how come you're out here, and she's stuck in there?"

Slowly, the smile slipped away. "Elements beyond my control. Let's leave it at that."

"The newspaper Andrew found spoke of five families murdered. The children stolen from those families were the rest of us, weren't they?" I fired relentlessly, goose bumps appearing across my arms as I recalled the discovery.

Demitra pushed back from the table, and got up collecting some cutlery and glasses and turning away from me to put them in the sink. Though I couldn't see her face, I could tell she was shaking—with anger or fear, I didn't know.

"I think you need to back off, Evelyn," she said. "Focus on getting your friends safe before you go rooting around."

"Why?" I pushed, braver with every word. "You expect me to go along with everything you say without questioning it, but so far, you haven't told me what Boundary even *is*. Why is everyone so bent on hiding the truth?"

"Because," Demitra said, still not facing me, "if you knew the truth, you might stop working with us."

"That's supposed to reassure me?"

Demitra picked something up out of the sink, and there was an odd crunching sound. "It's supposed to get you to evaluate your priorities. You need us just as much as we need you, if not more." She turned around, and I saw with some horror she'd crushed one of the drinking glasses in her hand. Blood trickled down her wrist from a nasty gash in her palm, glittering shards still embedded in her skin. "Don't go searching for a reality you can't handle yet."

I stared at her hand, trying to free my words from a tangled web of frustration. "I can handle it. I'm not weak, you know."

"But you have a conscience." Demitra's eyes fell to her palm with a dull realization. She threw the remnants of the glass into the sink with a crash. "Anyway, enough of that. You should get on and practise—"

All of a sudden she stopped, as if I'd interrupted her. Her eyes glazed over, body growing rigid, and for a moment I panicked that something terrifying had risen behind me. After a few seconds, the moment passed, and she relaxed.

"Deio needs me to come and get him," she said without further explanation. "We'll be back in ten minutes. Don't go anywhere."

Demitra wiped her hand, threw her shawl over her shoulders, and slipped out of the flat, leaving the door gaping open behind her. As I moved to shut it, I considered leaving to find Andrew. I could tell him I was right about Penny, and perhaps we could go to the library and do more research together.

Don't go searching for a reality you can't handle yet... If you knew the truth, you might stop working with us.

My hand hovered over the handle, deliberating. It wasn't like I was doing anything useful waiting in the flat. Unless, of course...

I shut the door, and tiptoed over to another one: the door to Deio and Demitra's bedroom. Tentatively, I rattled the knob, and wasn't particularly surprised to find it locked. My face flushed with guilt, I did a quick round of the flat searching for a key under the settee, and behind cushions and books, all in vain.

"Okay, Evelyn, think," I murmured to myself. "It's locked for a reason. You have ten minutes at best to get in."

Learning about my family had awoken a new hunger within me for the truth, one I had possessed but kept subdued for too long. If I was playing with my friends' lives, I wanted to make absolute certain I had the right people on my team.

But how to get in? I couldn't force it, and I hadn't the slightest idea how to pick locks. Penny and Avery could have figured it out, but not me. Fred and I especially were always useless at breaking the rules.

Thinking about him brought a new bout of panic, followed by a very idiotic idea. According to Demitra, I could control the Others. The Others, as far as I knew, weren't restrained by physical limitations of this world.

Open the door... Open the door...

I felt a bit silly, standing there with my eyes scrunched into slits and shouting with my mind. The longer I stood there, the more scared I became that Deio and Demitra would walk in on me.

Come on, please! Unlock the door!

I realized I was shaking. A clammy sweat broke out on my arms—I felt exhausted. My mind was starting to spin.

UNLOCK THE DOOR!

I flooded all my nervous energy into that one final cry. At once, a static pressure rushed past me, increasing my dizziness until my head spun out of control and I collapsed. However, when my vision cleared again, I noticed new cracks had appeared in the plaster of the ceiling—and the bedroom door was open a tiny crack.

"Yes!" I exclaimed, hurrying to my feet and bursting through the door.

After all that energy, I have expected something much more fantastic than what I found on the other side. Two narrow beds sat at opposite walls, the blankets heaped in the middle all torn, along with the pillows, which had feathers spilling out. The small window was broken too, as was the light bulb, and the wooden panels had all but been ripped off the walls. Perhaps I had been expecting a massive book labelled SECRETS or something, but I was a bit disappointed at the sheer normality of it. Well, despite the fact it was in shambles. Had the Others just done this, or was it always in such disarray? If it was the former, I was done for. There was no way I'd be able to tidy it all up in time.

Stop it, I chided myself. Focus. You don't have time to worry.

There really wasn't anything unremarkable about the room, nothing, which was clearly suspicious. There was a wardrobe, but the skewed door revealed the contents to be but a few simple garments. The mattresses looked too thin to be much use at hiding anything. My eyes fell on a small bedside table sitting between the two beds—a wooden cube with three drawers that were, oddly enough, properly closed.

Kneeling down, I tried the top drawer. It gave off a slight static shock, but apart from that, I managed to pull the entire thing out without resistance. I let the contents fall into my lap, heart in my mouth.

It was all photographs, many smudged and even more cut out of newspapers, and they were of different people. I couldn't imagine why the siblings had collected such a large amount of pictures of people: men, women, and children. They didn't even come from this world, this layer. At least I didn't think so. A few photos had hastily scrawled names, notes, or even addresses on the back, but most of it had been scribbled back out again so that I couldn't make out the words.

I sifted through to see if I recognized anyone, but they all remained perfect strangers to me. So I tried the second drawer.

I found a notebook. It was the only object in there, as big as a textbook, spiral bound and containing thick pages, almost all of which had been written on. When I flipped it open, it became apparent that all it contained were names. Names, addresses... and a single word penned in bold capitals. They were the same words repeated over and over again for different people: RIPPER, SENSER, and ASSOCIATE. Nearly every name was crossed out, and by the looks of things, they were alphabetically organized.

I flipped to the F section, scanning the page until I found the name I was looking for.

Penny Farthing **RIPPER** *Boundary.*

It wasn't crossed out. Underneath, there were the names

Bernard and Elisabeth Farthing, both crossed out, with the word ASSOCIATE by their names. I paged to the S section, heart starting to beat really quickly now.

Evelyn Stuart **SENSER** *accounted for.*

Not crossed out, but that wasn't the thing that caught my eye.

Robert and Elle Stuart **ASSOCIATE** *Maidstone, Kent,* crossed through.

Crossed out — deceased. I wondered if their pictures were in the first drawer? I blinked back tears, then suddenly turned back to where I had seen Penny's name in surprise.

Beatrix Farrington **RIPPER** *Boundary,* crossed out, needless to say, as she was deceased, was written right above *Madon Farrington* **RIPPER** *Unknown.*

I flipped through the pages for any other names I recognized, noting in dull surprise that nearly every single name was crossed off, enough so that the ones that remained stood out quite blatantly. Fred Ashton only had a question mark by his name, as did Lucas Reading, and Tressa McGinley. Avery Sadler was marked as a RIPPER. Around their names, there was a list of people from their families, all crossed through.

I was transfixed. Who else hadn't been crossed out? Almost everyone still alive was either a SENSER or ASSOCIATE.

Harriet Pearson **SENSER,** *Frome, Som.*

Anna Pearson **ASSOCIATE** *Frome, Som.*

Julia Pearson **ASSOCIATE** *Frome, Som.*

Andrew Pearson **ASSOCIATE** *accounted for.*

Harriet and her family. They had Harriet and the Pearsons written in here amidst all these other gifted, and mostly dead people. Was this because of Harriet's gift, or because I'd involved them in this mess.

Dizzily, I sat back to absorb this information. Demitra and Deio had about a hundred people organized in this neat notebook, and had classified them according to their powers, and crossed out the ones who were dead.

As I flipped through the pages, a single note fluttered down.

Dear Mrs Lachlan,

It has come to our attention that your promised payment of £400 is still outstanding. Considering that over six months have passed since the job was completed, we are understandably angered by this breech in... People are starting to wonder why two thirteen-year-olds are alone, and we need the money to find a new place... We have spared you from the unfortunate incidents of a few years ago because of this agreement, and without your cooperation, steps will be taken. We will come for you. One week until...

Sincerely,
Deio and Demitra Farthing

I scanned it over several times. It was water damaged, so some of the ink had smudged, but the remaining fragments seemed to have enough weight of their own. A quick flip through the notebook to look for the name revealed that *Shannon Lachlan* **RIPPER** *London* had been crossed off.

I opened the third and final drawer and found a selection of different guns, knives, and other lethal weapons.

Mercenaries. The word came immediately to mind, a term they'd used during my literature class in school. Hired killers. They weren't getting the names out of nowhere, and they weren't listing them without a reason. They must have someone directing them. I knew they hadn't personally committed every murder in the book, since Beatrix's death was most definitely at Madon's hands, but I would bet that they'd carried out a good few of them. They were seventeen years old, and they were killers. I thought back to the alleyway and how Demitra had attacked those women...the Whatley's.

I dropped the book as if it had bitten me, feeling really

quite sick now. I rushed to the window and threw it open, vomiting into the street below, everything piecing together with devastating clarity.

Bella Whatley and her sisters, the ones who had attacked us in the streets that eventful night, had been avenging their father's death. Their father, who if I recalled from the notebook correctly, had RIPPER by his name. Demitra and Deio were going after people who could Rip, or who had some unique connection to the Others, and they were squashing the problem by killing them. Of this I was now certain.

That would mean my family, all our families, had died because they were gifted. For some reason, with us, they hadn't followed the regular pattern and disposed of us; we had ended up in Boundary.

"Evelyn?"

I dropped the notebook. Whipping around, I saw Deio and Demitra standing in the flat doorway, their faces holding the same expression of horrified disbelief as mine must do.

Chapter Sixteen

"How did you get in?" Deio spoke first, shrugging off his coat and walking over to where I was standing frozen. He frowned at his sister. "Didn't you lock the door?"

She nodded, her face pale. "And I sealed the drawers."

"Clearly you didn't."

"I did!" Demitra insisted shrilly, snapping out of her shock and coming to join us. "I promise."

Deio gave her a very condescending look. "You don't need to lie to me."

"I'm not!"

My eyes darted between them, the panic having calmed back down. My heart was still hammering, but a newer, stronger emotion was rapidly overcoming me: anger.

"The door was locked, actually," I said, and they both turned their attention back to me. "The Others unlocked it for me."

Colour worked its way back into Demitra's cheeks at an alarming speed. Deio, though, seemed less fazed.

"They did some redecorating by the looks of things," he said, peering past me into the wreckage. "I have to say, I'm impressed you managed it, Evelyn. That's promising."

"Impressed?" Demitra said incredulously, looking between Deio and me. "Impressed? I've only just told her to keep her nose out of our business, and then she goes and does something like this!"

The photographs were scattered over the floor, a hundred faces that were now reduced to nothing more than memories in a drawer. The notebook was open to a random page full of stricken names and the letters, which had condemned them, including those of my family.

"You're killers." I spoke with impressive calmness, considering the hatred beginning to boil within me. "These people didn't do anything. They were like you and me—different—but you killed them anyway. You or others killed my family too."

Demitra snatched the notebook away from me, her entire body quivering. "Stop it, Evelyn. You don't know—"

"That's where you keep sneaking off to, isn't it?" I pushed. "To track down those remaining people? Who's paying you now? Madon?"

"He's on our hit list, if you hadn't noticed," Deio interjected, quite conversationally. "We're not paid anymore. That system wasn't working out." He chuckled, as if he'd said something funny.

Demitra wasn't laughing. Her grey eyes were stormy, flashing with a fury that seemed to match mine. It wasn't directed at her brother, though.

"You need to tell me what's going on, or I'm leaving." I folded my arms.

"See, this is exactly what I told you would happen!" Demitra said shrilly. "How are we going to help your friends then, huh?"

"*Help* them," I scoffed, standing up and glaring at her. "We're all on your list! I don't know why saving my friends is so important to you, but it probably isn't good for the rest of us." Then it hit me. "You were barred from entering when I won, weren't you? If you bring the rest of us back into this world, you'll be able to knock six more names off your list once and for all."

My throat was tight. Wind from the broken window gusted in, picking up the photographs and tossing them around the room, taunting us with dead faces.

"Penny is our sister," Demitra growled through her clenched teeth. "Why would we—"

"Why would you want to kill Harriet Pearson?" I interrupted. "Why would we six be so special that you'd lock us away rather than kill us like the rest? I don't know, Demitra, but I do know that I won't work with you anymore."

I had to get out of here, out of this room, away from them. I had to find Andrew and tell him his family was in danger.

"We were barely two years old when you were put in Boundary," Demitra snapped. "How could we have locked you away or killed your families?"

I didn't want to listen to her. My eyes and head were swimming. I'd always known that the truth behind our past was darker than I'd care to admit, but I hadn't expected it to be this brutal. I felt like an idiot for having blindly followed them for so long.

I skirted around her to the door, my heart beating so quickly I thought it would fail me.

Demitra shouted at me to stop, grabbing at my arm, but I shook her off.

Wham. The door slammed shut with such force that the cracks in the ceiling spread further. Demitra's palm was outstretched, her eyes on fire. She could move the door, but she couldn't lock it, and I pushed it back open again.

"You can't leave!" she shrieked, as one by one the books from the shelf flew at my head.

I ducked, too wound up to focus on calling the Others to help me. So I ran, crouched over and with my hands on my head to shield it from the objects being hurled at me. Vaguely, I was aware of an odd pressure beginning to build up, of something strange whispering fuzzily in my ear...

Then pain hit me. 'Hit' was a bit of an understatement. This was more of a stab, and for a moment, I thought Demitra had thrown one of the knives that were in the lower drawer. It wrenched through my body, excruciatingly painful, and I stumbled over. It wasn't in one place, but all over. My arms, my legs, my torso, my head...they were all hurting. I couldn't see, and all I was aware of was someone screaming and the feeling of my body burning... Suddenly, I wasn't in the flat in Gloucester anymore, but in a manor house, crying because I'd refused to come to dinner one day and the Master had caught me.

"Demitra, stop it!" Someone else shouted.

"Get off me!"

"You're going to wreck the barrier even more. It isn't worth it."

As quickly as it had come, the agony stopped. I lay on the floor, gasping and trying to shake off one terrible memory.

"Evelyn?" Fred is standing over me, uncertain. "Are you okay?"

"Is He gone?" I choke, trying and failing not to cry. "I was only...I didn't feel very well, and I..."

"It's okay." Fred offers a hand, glancing over his shoulder to make sure the Master really has gone. "Remember what Lucas says — it's all in your head."

"Doesn't feel like it," I sniff.

"Don't feel, then," Tressa says, marching up behind us. "Don't let Him win."

Grabbing onto the side of the settee for support, I hauled myself to my feet. Deio was physical restraining Demitra. The flat looked like a bomb had gone off inside of it, every window had shattered and smoke billowed through the doorway. I could hear the landlord shouting.

Without hesitating further, I ran out the door. When I got halfway down the stairs, now clogged with a greasy smoke, I chanced a look back.

Demitra was leaning against the doorframe, eyes closed, and body shaking convulsively as if she were crying; but there was no trace of tears. Deio was just standing there, eyes glued on me. His lips were moving, whispering to his twin.

He mouthed the words. "Don't worry. She'll be back. They all come back."

* * *

"Andrew Pearson?" I asked walking into the cheap inn were Andrew was staying.

"He left a few minutes ago. Looking for a phone box, I think."

"Where would I find one of those, then, please?"

The innkeeper drew me a quick map on the back of a napkin, I thanked her, and left. I had also inquired about any vacancies, deciding that returning to the flat probably wasn't the brightest idea, but they were full. Most rooms were being used to house people displaced by the bombs in London, but since Andrew was a 'wounded veteran', she had made an exception.

Outside, it was a regular November day, overcast and chilly, but not raining.

I tried to summon some positivity, but couldn't. There was something heavy sitting in my stomach, something that refused to disappear. For the first time, I was questioning whether I was doing the right thing. Perhaps in Boundary, sheltered from this world of murderers and violence, they were safer, happier...

Like you were? a snide voice in my head asked. *When all you cared about was having a matching set of jewellery for dinner? When your entire world was no bigger than a single house and the forest around it, when everybody knew who you were and cared about you?*

People rushed past me, no one giving me a second glance. Even now there were no boundaries separating us, we were still worlds apart.

I leant against a derelict building, head in my hands, wondering why I couldn't cry.

Chapter Seventeen

The phone box had peeling, faded red paint, and was panelled on all sides with mucky glass. Inside I could just make out the phone and black box, which had a couple of buttons. I'd never used one myself. It looked scary. Andrew was speaking into the handset.

"I don't...it isn't as easy as that. I'm sorry. Come on, Mum, don't hang up, I—" He suddenly frowned and replaced the handset.

"Hello," I said, opening the door, and he jumped.

"Evelyn, are you all right? You look..." He trailed off, unable to find the right word.

"They're assassins, Andrew," I said simply. "They kill people like me. Like Harriet. People who can Rip, or who are in tune with the Others, as well as their families. And Penny is their sister, I was right about that. I confronted them, and...I can't go back to them, Andrew, I can't."

Andrew had an odd look on his face. It seemed somewhere between relief and anger. "Thank God. But Harriet..."

I didn't know what to say. If the Farthings decided to come for Harriet and her sister, I couldn't think of anything we would be able to do to save them. My only hope was that by running away, they'd have more important things to think about.

We moved out of the telephone box, walking down the street in no particular direction.

"That was Mum on the phone," Andrew said eventually. "I had to tell her I was okay. She was about to rally the entire county into a search party. She thinks I've run away with you—I've never heard her so furious."

"I'm sorry."

He folded his arms, exhaling so that his breath fogged up the air. "She wants me back for Christmas. It's the first of December in less than a week."

"Are you going to go?" I asked dully.

We rounded a corner. The general store had a long queue outside it, packed with women and old men sifting through their ration books. Where was I going to eat now? I hadn't any idea how the system worked.

Andrew avoided looking at me. "I don't know what else to do, Evelyn. We've found Deio and Demitra, but obviously they aren't going to help you. You can't get your friends out of Boundary by yourself, but I can't afford to stay here much longer. Mum needs me. And yet..."

"And yet?"

And yet, I didn't want to face the alternative, the life where I tried to repair bonds with Julia, and stayed with her until I learned enough to make it on my own. The life where I accepted I would never see my friends again, and tried to forget Demitra's revelation that Penny was slowly but surely letting monsters filter into our world. The life where I ignored the fact I'd grown up in a parallel world for an unknown reason, and understood I would never know the truth.

"Andrew?"

"Mm?"

"Anna isn't like Harriet, is she? She's...normal?"

Andrew gave a dry laugh. "Yes. Although I'm not entirely sure how 'normal' can be defined anymore. Or what she might be hiding. Why?"

I just shrugged, not wanting to worry him. Not when there wasn't anything to be done about it.

After a good while of aimless wondering, we found an empty bench outside a derelict café. We sat and I picked up one of the pamphlets papered to the seat, blotted and crumpled with wear, a strong red caption screaming: *Hitler will send no warning—so always carry your gas mask!*

We'd had these at the school, and everyone hated carrying

theirs around. Most people on the streets carried theirs in little brown boxes at their side, and suddenly, I felt awfully exposed for having left mine behind. It was like a virus, the fear of war: it hadn't bothered me for most of my time here, but all of a sudden, I could feel the paranoia seeping into me, all consuming. That mechanical birds—planes—would come from the cruel land across the sea and kill everyone with a single push of a button. That the older men in smart uniform would snatch Fred and the other boys away from me the second I saw them again and throw them into one of those very planes to drop similar bombs on other people. That any moment, Demitra and Deio would come for me and push me in front of an oncoming car, or put a bullet in my brain and curl my fingers around the trigger. I remembered being back at Boundary with Demitra, and seeing it all materialize out of the mist. The peacefulness of the ancient trees, the soft and crumbling brick of the manor, the laughter of harmless tricks played on one another...I never wanted to leave. *Why did it have to be me?*

"Selfishly, I'm glad it was," Andrew said, and I realized I'd spoken aloud.

I shook my head vehemently. "You didn't know me then. I was..." Stupid? Ignorant? Shallow?

Happy?

"I was speaking to someone else before I called Mum." Andrew spoke again after I remained silent. "The librarian found her number for me. She thinks I'm doing research for a census or something. Anyway, I'm hoping you know who Beatrix Farrington is?"

"Was," I corrected, tears prickling in my eyes at the mention of her name.

"I found her sister."

"You did?" It was strange to think Beatrix had a family outside Boundary. "What did she tell you?"

"Nothing important, unfortunately." Andrew cringed as a

woman shouted at him from across the street, something along the lines of 'coward'. "She's in her sixties, training as a nurse at the moment in Kent. I tried ringing her, but the line was dead, so I'll have to try again later. Maybe it's a long shot, but better than nothing. Every connection counts, right?"

I pictured her name struck off that list, her black gravestone covered with snow, slowly sinking into the earth...

"Why are you doing this?" I asked, pulling my feet onto the bench and hugging my knees to my chest. I was freezing, wearing only a shirt, thin overcoat, skirt, and worn silk stockings. Here in the shade, there was even frost on the ground.

"I'm sorry." His face fell. "I shouldn't have brought her up."

"No, not that." I wound a strand of hair around my finger, as tightly as possible. "Why are you helping me? This has nothing to do with you, and it's just causing you trouble. We're dealing with murderers, Andrew."

"Because I want to."

I sighed. It wasn't the answer I was looking for, but I didn't want to push too far. I didn't want him to realize that perhaps he'd be better off leaving me alone. It was selfish of me, but old habits died hard; I hated the idea of having to go through anything by myself.

"You're shivering up a storm over there," he remarked.

I scowled but didn't correct him. It wasn't as if there was anything to be done about it; I had nowhere to go, no money to buy extra clothes, and nothing for food. Like in the sea, I had to try to embrace the cold, let the numbness spread...

"Have you, though? Missed me? You haven't done anything to try to bring us back. They nearly gave up on you, Evelyn."

I stood up so fast that a thread from my skirt wrapped around a nail in the bench, causing it to tear. I unhooked it. "What are we *doing?*" I asked, throwing my arms around in desperation. A lady who had been walking towards us with her children hastily crossed the street. "There has to be something we can do, anything! I'm not ready to give up just yet, I'm—"

"It's not giving up," Andrew interjected gently. "Not when you've reached a dead end."

"Have we, though? Reached a dead end?" I shook my head despairingly, wishing I could come up with ideas the way the others had been able to do. "Surely there has to be some way to back out and start again, find a new lead. Demitra said they're going to destroy themselves if we wait any longer."

Andrew's face grew stony. "Demitra is a murderer. She was lying to you."

I shook my head again, and began to pace. "She wasn't lying. Not then, anyway. I have powers, Andrew, I just don't know how to use them safely. I could make a difference, I just..." I trailed off, another memory pulling itself back into the light.

"I can see you're still beyond reason. I'll let you be for now if you promise to push Demitra about your past. She's evasive because she has so much to hide. Secrets that would send you running back to me."

I hated it. I hated the thought that Madon was right. I hated what it would force me to do. But I'd only seen one side of the story, and despite how unpleasant I was certain the other side would be, it was better than giving up. All I had to do was hear him out, no promises, no allegiance.

"Evelyn?" Andrew frowned at me, probably confused by the strange look that had come over my face. "What is it?"

"He killed Beatrix," I said slowly, "and I would never ever work with him. But he might have answers."

"What are you talking about?" He was worried now.

"Madon," I said, cringing at the name.

"You can't be serious."

"Just this once, I think I am."

"You're mad."

"Possibly."

Now it was Andrew's turn to get to his feet, pacing up and down the sidewalk with his ungainly limp. "Do you have a death wish? You might as well just go back to the Farthings for all the good that will do. You told me what he was like with you inside Boundary, what makes you think he'll be any different here?"

I inhaled through my teeth, ignoring the part of me that agreed with him. "Demitra used the Rips to torture. Just like him. Back in Boundary, it was they who started the fire, which trapped Fred. Deio made Avery stab Tressa. They created a word puzzle to distract Lucas. The only reason they helped Penny was because she's their sister, and the most likely to join with them after she escaped. I don't think Madon was as in control as he led us to believe, and that just might be the key to everything. He knows I hate him, so he doesn't have my trust to lose if he tells me the truth."

There, I'd said it. I'd either summoned the courage to free my friends, or I'd deluded myself to the point of suicide.

For what seemed like a very long time, Andrew didn't say anything. His flaxen hair, in desperate need of cutting, was half obscuring his face thanks to the bitter wind. No matter how hard I scrutinized him, I had no idea what was running through his mind.

"All right," he said finally. There was no humour in his tone, nothing light. "But I'm going home." I started to protest, but he held up his hand and continued. "Not because I'm abandoning you, but because I want you to come back with me. We'll take a break from all this madness, celebrate Christmas just like ordinary people, and then take it from there. You need a chance to think. We both do."

My eyes fell on the posters covering the bench again, like dead leaves in the autumn. Yes, I desperately wanted some normality again, even if it was with a family who probably hated me now. I wanted Julia's comfort, Kitty's goodwill, and James's innocence to surround me, not the negativity of the Farthings and Madon. The reality, however, was that I didn't have the time. Of that I was certain. This wasn't a game I could opt out of at will.

"Okay." I forced a smile, shuffling my feet to keep warm and wishing that I had some gloves. "Um, I suppose you'll need to pack?"

He nodded. "I know we didn't bring much, but everything counts nowadays."

"My things are back at their flat."

"But maybe exceptions can be made," he added. "Do you want to come back with me? I think I have some of Mum's humbugs sitting in a pocket there, if you're hungry."

It wasn't really a question. Where else would I go?

I feigned another smile. "Do you have enough money left for a bus?"

"No. But we'll find a way."

We made our way back down the street in a heavy, contemplative silence. Inwardly, though, I was shouting, throwing all the emotion I could into each word.

I know this is crazy, but I need you to call Madon. I don't know if this will work, but he said it would, so...call him. Call Madon.

Chapter Eighteen

I barely recognized the girl in the mirror. It was cracked, grimy, and cast with appallingly dim light, which didn't help her case, but I had a feeling it wasn't lying by much. Her black hair hung limply around her shoulders, the curls dragged down by weeks of inattention. Her clothes were shabby and dirty, her complexion sallow and unhealthy. Her eyes looked massive against protruding cheekbones: she was far too thin for what was considered attractive. Her name was Evelyn Stuart, but I didn't know her.

Andrew was in trouble with the innkeeper. He'd come up a few shillings too short, and she wasn't letting him into his room until he'd found the money. I'd heard her threaten to call the police.

I was in the lobby doing nothing. My head was pounding with excruciating force, and I had nothing to add to Andrew and the innkeeper's argument. If anything, I was glad for the stall: I wanted to wait until I was certain my call to Madon had failed. My gut feeling was that going back to the farm was wrong, and every obstacle that got in our way seemed to be fate's method of agreeing. What if I was leading the Farthings right back to Anna and Harriet? What if, what if, what if...

I tore myself away from my reflection, disgusted.

I kept throwing anxious glances to the hotel doors. Any minute, Demitra or Deio could come bursting in, realizing that I was contemplating switching sides, and kill me before I had a chance to do such a thing. Or worse, Madon. Half of me hoped my message had been futile.

"Miss, are you all right?" A young woman, heavily pregnant, came tottering down the stairs towards the doors. "You look like you're about to pass out."

"I'm fine," I said unconvincingly, clenching my fists to stop them from shaking. "Really."

She gave me a sympathetic smile. "My husband's in North Africa. Left just a week before I realized we were having a baby. They'll be home soon, though. Next Christmas, it'll all be different."

It took me far too long to realize she was referring to the war. She hurried on.

I sat down on the floor, with my back pushed up against the grimy inn wall. Andrew was fully immersed in his conversation with the innkeeper, the two of them growing louder by the second, and without much sign of stopping anytime soon. So I closed my eyes.

I dreamt of a cliff somewhere, enveloped in a thick fog so that the bottom was shielded from view… There were voices from the other side of the chasm, pleading for me to jump, but I knew that I could never make it—it was too far and I couldn't see them. Behind me, something was coming, but I couldn't turn around, transfixed as I was to the voices from the other side screaming for me to jump.

Evelyn! Evelyn! You have to come!

One eye flickered open. The shouts were so loud.

Evelyn?

Or more of a whisper, actually. So close that I had to whip my head around to make sure there was no one standing directly behind me in the wall. No. Andrew was still engaged with the innkeeper, and the lobby was otherwise deserted. I must have dreamed it.

Evelyn.

I leapt to my feet, glancing about wildly. The voice was speaking right in my ear, but there was absolutely nobody around whom it could have been.

Evelyn.

It was drifting away now. Without thinking, I took a step forward, searching. Yes, there it was, whispering away by the door. When it began fading again, I followed it out of the door, not even pausing to tell Andrew where I was going—I didn't really know myself.

I was halfway down the street before I realized that it was probably Madon's doing. I was totally unarmed and alone (not that I knew how to defend myself anyway). The whispers grew louder as I hesitated, so squashing any reservations, I followed them away from the heart of the bustle. Away from the more affluent commercial district into an area of ugly, cheap townhouses, littered with rubbish and narrow alleys. Night had nearly fallen, turning the sky a deep navy and plunging the temperatures to near freezing, but I was at the point where I couldn't get any colder. Perhaps that was why I wasn't afraid; I was just numb.

Evelyn?

I must have walked for two to three miles. The soles of my feet were beginning to ache. The whispers finally stopped around an abandoned children's playground, consisting of a metal slide and swing set in the middle of a leafy park. There weren't any streetlamps nearby, and once I stopped near the swings, I noticed exactly how dark it was.

At last, I began to panic.

"Oh, no." The whispers had faded, and feeling was flooding back. "Blast..." I began to shiver.

I began walking as fast as I could back to the road, wondering why I'd let the voices carry me this far into nowhere, when I noticed the silhouette of another person rapidly making their way towards me.

It wasn't Madon. Madon had a certain elegance in the way he moved, and this man (he was wearing trousers) possessed none of that.

I tried to concentrate and feel for the Others, but I was too scared to think coherently. Anyway, what would I make them do?

Oh Lord, he was getting closer. He must have called me here, somehow, but I didn't want to talk to him. Not here, not without anything or anyone for protection.

As casually as possible, I turned and began walking across the park in the opposite direction. Then the panic took over and I began running.

"Evelyn, wait!"

How did he know my name? He was probably working for Madon, like Bella and her sisters had been. What if he was working for the Farthings?

My shoes were slipping off, so I kicked them away and kept running barefoot. I could hear the rapid footsteps of him chasing me, and by the sound of it, gaining ground. The road wasn't too far away now, and I could see the hazy figures of people moving about in their homes...

Think.

My stockinged feet slipped on a frosty patch of grass, and I was thrown ungracefully to the ground. The man skidded to a halt behind me, panting just as much as I was.

"Get away!" I screamed, struggling back up. "I'll...I'll..."

"For God's sake, I'm not going to—"

I didn't wait around to hear. Kicking out I caught his leg and tripped him up. I heard him cry out in shock and pain. I jumped to my feet and not looking back, continued running.

He didn't follow, but shouted, somewhat dejectedly, "Evelyn, please! Don't you recognize me?"

Something in his voice stopped me. My heart was hammering so fast it was a wonder I was still alive, and every muscle in my body tensed up, as I prepared to flee again. Against my better judgement, I turned around and faced him.

He was dressed head-to-toe in strangely fashionable black clothing, tall and wiry without being particularly thin or muscular, and was somewhat in between. His hair was dark brown, much too long for the style of today, and hung limply around an almost-but-not-quite-handsome face.

He came closer, carefully, as though I was a deer or some frightened animal who was about to bolt.

The moment I saw his eyes I knew.

"Hello, Avery," I whispered.

Part Two

Chapter Nineteen

"Impossible. You can't...this isn't...why would you...?" I choked in between a sudden onslaught of tears. "Avery!"

"Believe it." He smiled weakly. "Why are you the one breaking down? I'm the one who has to deal with all this futuristic madness."

This only made me cry harder, hanging on to him as if I'd never let go. Everything that had been happening in my life suddenly seemed insignificant. Avery was here. Nothing else mattered.

"You've grown taller," I said with a watery grin, sniffing and hiccupping at the same time.

"That's what you notice?" He feigned hurt. "Not the newly revised wardrobe or the length of my hair? Besides, I should bloody well hope that I'm not the same height I was a year ago." I made a noise halfway between a laugh and a sob. Finally, I drew away, surveying him fully. He was certainly much, much taller, and his voice was quite a bit deeper. He was harder somehow, less boyish. But still Avery. Still Avery.

My mouth opened and closed, the sheer number of questions I needed to ask clogging up my ability to speak. Why, who, *how...*

I slipped my shoes back on and we drifted back towards the swings as the curtains of the surrounding houses began to twitch. We sat down on the damp wooden seats, letting the wind push us gently back and forth.

"Are you alone?" I asked eventually, focussing on my feet.

"Yes." He nodded. "Trust me, if it were possible to have brought everyone I would have done so. Well, maybe I'd have left Fred behind, since I know how much you hate him..."

I kicked him, but with not much force. "How is everyone, then?"

"Not good," he admitted, digging his shoes into the gravel so that his swing stopped moving. "Living any great period of time without Beatrix proved to be harder than we thought. Tressa nearly ran herself into the ground trying to get everything done; cooking, cleaning, gardening, mending clothes, all these things we used to take for granted. We never ran out of supplies, thank goodness, but it's a mess. The lawns are all overgrown, everything is filthy, and we are fighting all the time."

I remembered visiting, how some of the details had changed. I was glad the picture in my mind was still of the estate in its full glory, not this wasted vision Avery was painting.

"Penny wouldn't speak to me for about a month," he recalled offhandedly, brow furrowed at the memory. "She went through a spat with pretty much everyone at some point. Tressa was unbearable for quite a while too, though we all let her off because of the stress she was putting herself through. Lucas basically lives in the library trying to figure a way out, and Fred just hovers about like a little cloud; sometimes raining, sometimes bright and cheerful."

"Does he still...do they talk about me?" I choked.

"Fred? It's getting him to shut up about you that's the problem," Avery muttered with a small smile. "Of course we haven't forgotten you. Well, no less than you've forgotten us."

I flinched at the not-so-subtle dig, guilt nearly overpowering sadness.

"That they can't hold out much longer, is my point," he finished. "Which is where we come along."

"Do you know about the Others?" I inquired hoarsely, the vain part of me hoping he hadn't.

"I think. Vaguely."

So I told him absolutely everything. Unusually for him, he listened without once interrupting, and I could almost see him taking mental notes of what I was saying. Avery was the first person I'd come across from whom I didn't have to hide anything, and it felt as though a weight had been lifted from my shoulders.

"So you can control these things?" he asked when I'd finished, eyes wide with excitement.

"Not very well, but yes." I smiled proudly.

"I can Rip, but not very well either." He chuckled. "So between us, if two halves make a whole, we have a pretty good gift."

"You can?" I exclaimed, surprised. There was a lot which had gone on behind the scenes in Boundary, things I was just starting to understand.

"Not half as well as Penny. Or Tressa, for that matter." At my astonishment, he continued, "She only figured it out about four months ago. Lucas and Fred are still, well, normal. Maybe they're like you?"

Gosh, there were so many things I needed to say, to ask. I was a jumbled mixture of guilt, elation, and confusion. It didn't feel real, and I was terrified that I'd wake up and find myself back in that hotel lobby, Andrew shaking me awake and telling me it was time to leave. The very idea made me feel sick. Now I had Avery back, I didn't ever want to let him go.

"Your name is Sadler, by the way," I blurted, worried that if I stayed mute for too long he'd get up and walk away. "Avery Sadler."

He nodded slowly, but didn't say anything. The chains on his swing were sticky, creaking with even the slightest movement. "And you said Penny was D's sister?"

"Yes. Poor Penny."

"Depends on how you look at it." He shrugged. "I'm not entirely surprised; it was obvious they had some sort of connection."

"They killed our parents, Avery," I reminded him, listening to the rhythmic creaking of the swing. It was very hard not to completely break down again.

"No." Avery gave me a funny look. "How could they? Assuming we were taken when we were infants, they couldn't have been more than two years old themselves, according to your information."

"Right." Well, that wasn't a very bright observation, Evelyn, I thought. Which meant Madon...but that notebook...

"I can't tell if you've changed or not," he said eventually. "On the outside, and maybe a bit on the inside—but I think deep down, you're still the same you. That's lucky. Not everyone escapes with so much."

"Not even you?"

He just smiled.

After another bout of pensive silence, we began walking back into the city. I was still shivering and 'stole' Avery's jacket. I wondered what I was going to do once we re-joined Andrew.

"You couldn't have picked a location closer town?"

"I knew you'd be...ah, excited. I didn't want to make a scene, and this place is usually abandoned."

I digested that information slowly, and said, "Wait, how long have you been here?"

"A day. I'm still getting used to it."

"Then how did you know about all this?" I gestured. "Who's helping you? And how...how did you get out in the first place."

Hands shoved into his pockets, Avery acted as if he hadn't heard me, quickening his pace so that I had to skip to keep up. I grabbed his arm, pulling him back until he stopped.

"What?" he asked innocently.

"What did you do?" I snapped, staring right into his eyes. "How did you get out, Avery?"

He muttered something under his breath.

"Excuse me?"

"I made a deal with Madon, all right?" He shook me away in exasperation. "He couldn't stay for more than a few minutes at a time inside the Boundary after you left, but he managed to... Oh, don't look at me like that! It is what it is, and I'm here now."

"You just left them there."

"And who does that remind me of?"

"I didn't have a choice!" I shouted.

"Didn't you?" Avery was smiling, but without any humour. "Face it, Evelyn, we both did what we had to. Madon got me out, helped me adjust, and all I have to do is help him with something that won't affect us at all. I'm learning things from him I'd never learn anywhere else, and once I've gathered enough information, you and I can rescue the rest of them. And," he added when I began to interrupt, "correct me if I'm mistaken, but you were the one calling for a meeting with him only a short time ago?"

I glanced down at my hands, wishing for the umpteenth time that they'd stop shaking. This was all so overwhelming. It would be extremely hypocritical of me to begrudge Avery his freedom, but I was furious with him for not bargaining a way out for all of them. Still, the reality was that only the Farthings and Madon held any answers, and neither of them were exactly 'perfect allies'.

"He called me here tonight, didn't he? That wasn't you?"

"Yeah, I assume so. He's changed a lot, hasn't he? Madon, I mean. He seems so—"

"Human?" I offered.

"Exactly. And desperate." Avery laughed. "Makes a nice change."

We began walking again. There was something aimless about it, as if neither of us really had any idea where we were going. Yet, somehow, I felt...happy. If Avery could leave Boundary, then there was a glimmer of hope that we could also save the others without incident. Together, we'd be able to do it; Avery was my key to escaping this dead end.

"Can you promise me something?" Avery said when we were nearly back at the hotel.

"Of course. What is it?"

"Don't tell anyone about me. And when I say anyone, I mean it." He was uncharacteristically serious. "Not even people you trust."

I was confused. "But Andrew will want to know who you are?"

We stopped outside the hotel at last, quite some time after I'd left. The lights were all off, but that didn't mean anything with the blackout.

Avery took a step away from me. "I-I'm not coming with you, Evelyn. I can't. I've promised Madon—"

"What?" I felt a familiar panic begin to rise.

"I owe him a favour now, that's all. But he said that D—the Farthing twins—can't know what happened, or they'll..." He gestured. "I don't know. Blow me up. Blow us all up."

"Andrew can keep a secret."

Avery hesitated, invisible in the darkness. "But if I come with you, won't the Farthings—"

"I want nothing to do with them anymore," I retorted. "You can't just leave me!"

"But I'd forgotten how irritating you were," he joked—at least I hoped he was joking—coming to stand next to me again. "Though I suppose sticking together might be the best thing. You've got to *promise* me that this Andrew won't say anything to the Farthings, all right?"

"Of course. You'll like him, he's...well, he's been kind to me."

"I'm sure," Avery said, in a tone that sounded too dry to be sincere.

"Be nice."

He rolled his eyes and crossed his heart, then moved to open the doors into the hotel. I followed him inside, still unable to grasp that Avery was *here*, and that I would never have to worry about being misunderstood or abandoned again.

Chapter Twenty

"What do you mean, gone?"

"I mean exactly that." The receptionist snapped her guest book shut, glaring at me over the wire rims of her glasses. "Gone. No longer here. Departed. I believe the French say *disparu.*"

"But he said—"

"My dear, what he *said* has no consequence. Your young man is no longer here, we are no longer accepting new guests, and so your presence is accomplishing nothing for either of us. Good night."

She waited for me to leave. When I didn't move she shuffled away from the desk, sucking loudly on her teeth in obvious irritation.

Andrew was gone. Judging by the clock, I'd been away for under two hours, yet he hadn't waited for me. He'd left for the farm without leaving so much as a note, a hint, *anything*.

"I don't understand," I said to Avery, heart hammering. "Why didn't he wait?"

"Sounds like a bit of a rubbish friend."

"He's not," I shot back. "He's probably just..."

My words fizzled into nothing.

There was nowhere else Andrew had a connection with in Gloucester, and certainly nowhere else that he might have gone to meet me. He wouldn't have rushed off to deal with an emergency, as news just didn't travel that fast from the country, yet why else would he disappear without telling me? Where else would he have gone?

"Evelyn?"

"Demitra's flat," I whispered. "It's the only other place we ever went to. Maybe he left something behind. Maybe he thought I'd gone there."

"You're reaching," Avery said, not unkindly. "Maybe he's wandering around trying to find you? I mean, you left without telling him where you were going, and if he's half the knight you make him out to be, I doubt he decided to sit around and just wait."

But Andrew wasn't stupid. Trying to find someone in a city, in the thick of blackout, would have been as effective as groping for peas in lentils whilst blindfolded. Like him, there were only two clear places I would have gone to anyway, here again, or the flat.

"Where are we going?" Avery skipped to catch up with me.

"The flat," I said, picking up my pace. My feet were burning from so much walking in one night, the soles of my shoes wearing thin.

He stopped.

"Are you mad?"

"I need to make sure—"

"I can't go with you," Avery said, although he'd begun walking again. "And besides, if he forgot something there, he'll be back at the hotel soon. This is stupid."

She'll come back. They always do.

Maybe I was being irrational, but the moment I'd realized Andrew was missing, a dread had settled into my bones that I couldn't shake.

It will take three to save your friends. No more, no less.

Demitra and Deio needed me, one way or another. Within Boundary, they'd proven they had no problem with using our relationships to manipulate us. Andrew was my undisputed best friend in this world.

And if there was one thing life had taught me so far, it was that nothing was too far-fetched to be true.

"I still can't come with you." Avery peered up at the flat, hovering behind an unlit lamp post. "And I still think you're being stupid."

"Surprise, surprise," I snapped. It was amazing how fast the high of seeing him had faded; it almost felt like we'd never been apart. Despite what he claimed, I decided he hadn't changed much at all. "Stay outside if you want."

He grumbled something unintelligible.

My hands were shaking, so it took several tries to insert the key into the lock. Exhausted, cold, and overwhelmed, trying to prepare for what I'd say to the twins proved to be impossible. With luck, they'd be asleep, and might not even notice me.

"Urgh, it reeks in here," Avery muttered from directly behind me, raising a hand to cover his nose. "What is this? It smells like a stomach ache feels."

"Grease. I thought you weren't coming?"

"Yeah, well," he wrinkled his nose, "thinking about it, I never did give a damn about Madon's rules. And I don't want to deal with Fred if you die due to my negligence." He said it so casually, as though there was no question about us seeing him again.

"Okay. Just don't go getting yourself hurt either."

I went first up the stairs, wincing with each creak.

I'm not here to apologize. I'm not here to make amends. I want...

The door to the flat was already open. No lights glowed from within. It was silent, but not the peaceful sort; the kind of silence that set your ears ringing and made the room feel a hundred times smaller.

"They're not here," I whispered, not needing to double check. "Nobody's here."

"You sure they aren't asleep?"

I didn't answer, tiptoeing inside. It was too dark to make out even silhouettes of furniture, so after making sure the blackout blind was closed, I groped about for the light switch.

The overhead bulb flickered, once, twice, before casting a gloomy orange glow about the place. Immediately, it became apparent I was right.

The furniture was gone: the cabbage-rose settee, the bookshelves and their contents. The rug, the lampshade, even the dishes. The floorboards were marked with scratches as though the heavier furniture had been pushed a certain distance before its disappearance. Only a single mug remained, sitting on the kitchen countertops with an inch of greyish tea pooling in the bottom.

Avery exhaled. "Thank goodness."

I whirled on him. "This isn't right. Andrew vanishes, *they* vanish, and the flat is wiped clean...it's—something has obviously—" I choked back the hysterics. "They've taken him, Avery, don't you see?"

"No. All I see is an empty flat."

The bedroom turned out to be vacant too, including that damning chest of drawers.

"But why would they take the furniture?" Avery asked from the sitting room, still sounding sceptical. "If I were to kidnap someone, taking the cutlery wouldn't be my number one priority. You'd think it'd slow them down."

"I don't know," I shouted, loud enough that he flinched. "Sorry. I just—I have a terrible feeling about this."

"It's strange, I'll give you that." He grinned. "Although I've seen stranger. Deep breath, Evelyn."

I stood motionless in the doorway, watching dust mites flitter in and out of sight around the light bulb. For a moment, that was all I could register.

"I've got to call her."

"Who?"

"Demitra. With the Others, like..." I swallowed. "Just to make sure."

"From what you've told me, that doesn't sound like your best idea." Avery sat down with his back to a wall and motioned for me to join him. "It's gone midnight. Make a decision in the morning."

"I can't just go to sleep!"

"Sure you can." He yawned. "Besides, if they did take your friend, you'll soon hear about it. There'd be no point for them otherwise."

I was past the point of tiredness by now, my eyes burning and my brain spinning and panicking and offering no practical advice. Avery, rare as it was, was right. So I curled up in a corner by the window, acutely away of every nail and splinter in the floorboards.

Avery is here. Andrew is not. Killers live in this room. There's a war outside. You need three, you have two, and time is tick, tick, ticking.

* * *

"No water," Avery muttered, turning the taps on and off again. Each turn let loose a screech.

I cringed. "Can you stop?"

"Headache?"

I nodded and immediately regretted it. The room spun.

"There *is* tea." He picked up the mug and sniffed it. "Want some?" When I didn't reply, he shrugged and downed it in a single gulp, pulling a face. "That's *foul.*"

Still sporting an expression as if he'd swallowed a bucket of maggots, Avery crossed the room and began to raise the blackout blind, washing the place with daylight.

"Why'd you do that for?" I whined, shielding my eyes.

"When was the last time you ate?"

The mere idea of food sent my stomach writhing. "I think...I think I had a pickled-onion sandwich yesterday morning."

"Is there one of those grocery shops nearby?" He seemed proud of himself for remembering the correct term. "We could get some cereal or pastries."

"No money or ration tickets. Anyway, no money."

"Looks like we're licking grease off the walls downstairs, then."

I forced a smile. A quick glance proved there was no point in trying to straighten out my clothes, and I wasn't even going to bother checking my hair. The side of my face was smarting, the shape of the wood grain imprinted into my cheek.

Come to me.

"Would it help if I opened the window? Tressa used to say that— What are you *doing*?" Avery cried.

"I need the Others," I said. "I need to get Demitra, remember?"

The room began to fill with a buzzing pressure, the light bulb swinging as though in a gentle breeze.

"Don't," he said, urgently. "If you're right and they took him, then this is what they'll want: for you to retaliate."

"There's no other option."

"Get Madon instead."

Surprised, my concentration broke, and the rushing stopped. "Why?"

"You were going to anyway, weren't you? He can't hurt us here. He's the only person who might know what they're up to."

I hesitated. "You're...you're sure?"

Avery nudged open the window, turned back to me, and shrugged. "What do we have to lose?"

As ever, that loaded question.

I closed my eyes, tried to ignore the throbbing within my skull, and concentrated on Madon's name, over and over again.

Call him. If you're there, call Madon.

How long would it take? It wasn't as though the Others could let me know when they'd done their job—or if they'd done it at all—and even then, would Madon risk Ripping here? Would he even come to the Farthing flat? Would he assume it to be a trick?

Just when the pressure began to be unbearable, a different sort of shift happened—static, cold, and a stab of nausea.

When I opened my eyes, Madon stood in the doorway, even shabbier than he'd been last time.

"You called?" He looked at Avery, then back at me.

I'd been expecting Avery to speak first, and when he didn't, it took me an oddly long time to think of what to say.

"They're gone," I mumbled. "And so is Andrew."

"Clever girl."

He was mocking me. *Why did it have to be you, out of all of them? Pathetic.*

I curled my fingers into fists, straightening and trying my hardest to pretend my brain wasn't on fire. After all, I'd just called and used the Others flawlessly, and there was nothing pathetic about that; I was in control here.

"You know things," I said, clearer this time. "We need you to tell us where Demitra and Deio went, and we need you to help us find Andrew."

Madon stared at me, black eyes shining as if they were made of plastic. "And why would I do that?"

"You helped Avery. You're working against the Farthings, and we—"

"No, no, no," he snapped, overriding me. He stormed over to the bedroom, threw open the door, and surveyed the empty space with a sneer. "Cowards." Then he pivoted back to Avery and me, neither of us having moved, and said, "I didn't want you working with those twins, but it seems they've thrown you off all on their own. I helped Avery because I'll need a favour futher on down the road. That's as far as it goes. So long as you stay away from Demitra and Deio—away from Boundary—I couldn't give a damn what you do now. The last thing I have time for is helping you rescue some insignificant farm boy."

"He's not insignificant."

"He's another average human. The world is too full of them anyway—that's why they're killing each other in Europe at the moment. One more, one less." Madon began walking down the stairs to the shop. "What do I care?"

Avery continued to say nothing, frowning at the floor as though searching for a lost button. I jerked my head pointedly. He blinked, then hurried after me down the stairs.

"Why come? Why come if you won't help us anyway?" I

called.

Madon just kept walking.

The chip shop was dark, the windows having been boarded up when the shop closed down. Only a sliver of light worked its way down from the flat upstairs, illuminating the peeling whitewash walls and mouldy countertops of the front desk. By now, the smell didn't bother me.

"Why do you care if Boundary falls or not?"

Madon reached for the door handle.

Lock it. Lock the door.

"Evelyn?" Surprised flitted across his face as he rattled the handle. "You've become better."

"Answer my question."

As the pressure began to build again, I heard a pop as the bulb upstairs shattered, and the entire building was plunged into darkness.

"I can still Rip away," Madon said.

He was lying. I'd brought too many Others for Ripping to be safe.

I could feel them all swarming the building, invisible, lost—I knew I was the only thing stopping them from blowing the windows out again. The second I gave up control...

Madon must've realized this.

"You want to know why I need Boundary?" he asked, his voice managing to be both lilting and harsh at the same time. "You needn't look farther than this room. I am facing two children who used to be too scared to breathe my name, and now, when I look into your faces, I see anything but fear. In this world, I'm no better than the fools hiding behind submarines and machine guns. But in Boundary..." He paused. "There, I'm still a god."

My back grew rigid.

"That's it? That's why you won't help us?"

Avery, from somewhere behind me, snorted. "A devil, maybe. God probably isn't the right word."

My mind remained somewhere else. *Three.* If Madon cooperated, we'd be able to go to Boundary this minute and save everyone. By tomorrow morning, I could be holding Fred's hand as we searched for Andrew together, but because Madon wouldn't let go of the fantasy he'd created...

Something inside me snapped. Maybe it was still the shock of seeing Avery, maybe it was the headache, maybe it was the pressure of trying to control the Others, or maybe it was a combination of all of them, but at that moment, all my fears and anxieties were enveloped by a burning red rage.

I stretched my hand towards Madon.

He screamed as his body was thrown against the wall with such force that dust exploded from the ceiling. As the anger and pressure increased, the scream was choked off, replaced by a gargling wheeze.

"I can't torture you. Not like you tortured us," I managed to spit, struggling to keep him pinned down. "But believe me, I can still make it hurt."

"Avery..." Madon gasped. "Make her...stop."

Avery shook his head slowly, leaning against the opposite wall with a sideways smile.

Don't let up. Hold him there.

"You will tell us where Demitra and Deio are," I hissed. "You will tell us what you know about Andrew's whereabouts. If you truly know nothing, then you will help us anyway, or I swear on Beatrix's memory, I will let the Others kill you. I am *fed up* with dancing around a line in the sand. Understood?"

I barely understood myself. I knew I'd have to let up eventually, and I knew that my threat was empty, but I didn't care. I couldn't keep waiting for other people to make moves—I had to start making my own. Perhaps if I'd done so sooner, Andrew wouldn't be missing.

"You...have no idea..."

Harder.

The words slipped into a rattle.

"Careful," Avery murmured.

I withdrew the pressure, slightly.

"I felt...they Ripped to the farm. Last night. That's...all I know."

Let him go.

Madon collapsed onto the floor, gasping.

"The Pearson farm?" I demanded.

"Yes." He sounded angry; at himself or me, I couldn't tell. "Whether that boy is with them, I can't say."

Of course he was. Why would they go to the farm if it had nothing to do with Andrew?

"Take us there."

Madon put a hand on the wall and stumbled to his feet, laughing a hollow laugh. "You've made it far too unstable to Rip, my dear."

"I'll make them go away, but you've got to take us to the farm."

Another laugh. "And you trust me to do so? Have you not been listening? I cannot bring you right to the Farthings. And *he*—" Madon glanced at Avery— "would especially do well to keep his presence a secret from them."

"I just...I just need to make sure they're safe," I said, thinking of Julia and Kitty and Harriet with a biting guilt. "I don't want anything to do with the twins."

"Besides," Avery added, "we're going anyway. At least this way you'll be able to keep an eye on us."

Madon had been trying the door again, but at Avery's words, he straightened and frowned at us, thinking. I'd never known anyone to flip between being so unreadable and so violent in temperament as him. He'd been wrong about us not fearing him anymore; even now, my nerves were braced for an explosion of rage, or a punishment for being disrespectful.

"Fine," Madon snapped, much to my amazement. "But you've

got to clear all these *things* out of here, or the building will come down on top of us. You realize that as soon as I Rip, they'll know exactly where we are?"

"That's why you're coming, isn't it?" Avery retorted.

"Regrettably."

They both looked at me pointedly.

Hoping that I wasn't making a terrible mistake, I closed my eyes and willed the Others to leave.

Chapter Twenty-One

It was far more difficult getting the Others to leave than to come. Still, bit by bit, the pressure dwindled until I couldn't feel it anymore. I'd half-expected Madon to vanish the second he had the opportunity, but he must've taken Avery's threat seriously.

With precision even Demitra couldn't mirror, Madon opened a Rip in the middle of the shop as though dragging a knife through space itself. I didn't have time to reconsider before the world shifted and the smell of stale grease shifted into that of manure.

The farm.

Disoriented, it took me a minute to get my bearings. We were halfway down the driveway, surrounded by bare hedges and the wide expanses of frost-covered fields, the roofs of the house and barns visible if I stood on my toes. The air here felt colder than it had in town, making me even more aware of how threadbare my clothes were.

"Quaint," Avery said, his breath turning misty as he exhaled. "What's the plan?"

"Like I said, they'll know we're here." Madon fixed his coat and began walking down the driveway. "The family believes me to be a surveyor, so it isn't my presence that will cause a stir, is it?"

I gave Avery an 'I'll-explain-later' look. "We've got to find — well, anyone who isn't a Farthing, and find out if they've seen Andrew. Simple."

Of course, it wasn't simple at all. My departure hadn't been a smooth one, and if I showed up unannounced claiming that I'd lost Andrew, Madon would be the least of my problems.

I couldn't believe only a few days had passed since we'd left. I had the strangest sense of coming home, a flush of familiarity sparked by the twisting timber beams of the house and the frozen mud of the farmyard where I'd spent so much time doing chores. It wasn't quite as strong as the ache I associated with Boundary, but it was still there. The farm was the closest I'd come to belonging in this world.

"We should try the animal barns," I said. "That's where most of them will be at this time."

And by *them*, I meant the children. Harriet, Anna and James were a far safer bet than Julia.

Avery shrugged and nodded. Madon didn't respond, scanning for the twins.

"Oh!"

"What?" Avery started. "What is it?"

"The chickens," I said sadly, gesturing to the empty coop. "They're gone."

"And?"

"It's a shame. They were quite sweet little things."

Avery rolled his eyes. "I've been meaning to congratulate you on your newfound toughness, but now —"

"What, I can't be tough *and* empathize with chickens?"

Madon hissed at us to be quiet, cutting off Avery's response, and we walked the rest of the way in silence. Inside, though, I couldn't help but smile; there had been something genuine behind Avery's joke, and the idea of him thinking of me as 'tough', no matter how lightly, was flattering. After all, wasn't I the first of our group to actually outdo Madon face-to-face?

My smile faltered when, listening at the doors of the nearest barn, I heard Julia scolding someone, her footsteps growing louder and louder. We'd barely jumped out of the way when the door was thrown open and she emerged, as frazzled as ever, with a red-faced Anna at her heel.

"I can't do the work of a dozen people, Mum!" Anna shouted. "You're being unreasonable."

"Am I?" Julia spun around. If she'd bothered to look beyond her daughter, she'd have seen Madon, Avery, and I flattened in the shadows of the barn. "Is it too much to expect chores to be done properly, now?"

"I didn't—"

"We can't afford to waste anything. *Anything.* I know there aren't many of us, but we've got to..." Julia broke off. Her voice sounded strained, as though she'd been crying.

"Should we talk to her?" Avery muttered.

I shook my head, wishing myself to be invisible.

"I'll clean it up," I heard Anna say. "I-I'm sorry, Mum."

Julia waved her hand, turning away so I couldn't see her face. "I'll find the bucket."

We waited until they'd disappeared into the house to move again. I exhaled through my teeth.

"One day," said Avery, "you'll have to tell me this whole story in greater detail. Is it just me, or are you their villain?"

"Oh, shut up."

"I do wonder about you sometimes. Fred gets close, nearly dies in a fire. Andrew gets close, and *poof.* The chickens get close, and—"

"*Avery.*"

"Evelyn?"

I jumped, nearly cracking my neck due to turning so fast. For a blinding second I thought Julia had heard us talking and come back, until my eyes locked with Kitty's, except, it didn't look like Kitty. Her eyes, which I remembered to be wide and twinkling, stared at me listlessly, rimmed in dark, bruise-like bags. Her shoulders were slumped and her crooked smile was gone altogether.

"Kitty?" I stepped forwards, swallowing. "I—"

"Are you real?" she interrupted.

"What?"

"Are you real? See, I been muddled lately, and I wouldn't be surprised if you was just some of Harriet's ghouls." Her fingers flickered to her faded red headscarf, pulling at a loose thread. "So is it really you?"

"Of course. Kitty, what on earth happened?"

Her expression didn't change at my admission, her fingers continuing to pull the thread. I think she said something, but it was too muffled to hear.

"Why don't we go somewhere a bit...quieter?" I asked, hearing Julia and Anna's voices coming towards us. "Then you can tell me everything."

We ended up moving to a space behind the woodpile, hidden from view and far enough away from the main farmyard that nobody would be able to hear us. Madon stood to the side, still watching for the twins, but Avery, Kitty, and I kept close to the woodshed itself. A bitter wind was blowing across the fields, and the shed offered the slightest bit of shelter.

"Sidi Barrani," Kitty said tonelessly.

"I don't understand?"

"They won. They were outnumbered and outgunned, and they still won. It was an amazin' victory." Her lower lip trembled. "They lost fewer than seven 'undred men, which ain't bad. The Dutch lost three-an'-a-half thousand durin' their invasion, and the French lost somethin' like four-hundred-thousand. So, y'know, all things considered..."

My stomach dropped. "Your brother?"

Kitty nodded. Then her mask cracked and she began to cry, great gulping sobs. "I knew he was in North Africa, but...the battle wasn't supposed to be heavy with casualties...an' the last thing I told him was what I wanted for Christmas. Last thing he 'eard from me weren't that I loved 'im, but that I-I missed chocolate. An'...I *do* miss chocolate, but...oh, stars, Evelyn, I miss 'im more, an' he don't *know* that..." Her words trailed off into sobs and she buried her face in her hands, entire body shaking.

I reached out and patted her shoulder, trying not to cry myself. "I'm so sorry, Kitty."

"Y'know what the worst part it?" She raised her head, eyes red, swollen and glistening. "Life goes on like he never existed.

It didn't matter none, not to anyone else. Wouldn't have made no difference if he'd been in Egypt or...or Iceland, they'd 'ave won anyway. One more death, one less, would have changed nothin'."

Another gust of wind burst inwards from the fields, and I saw a slip of paper tumble from her blouse pocket. It was crumpled to the point of disintegration, but the words marked upon it were still legible:

Deeply regret to inform you that S/SGT B Rogers died of wounds sustained in Sidi Barrani on December 11th 1940. Profound sympathies offered.

"I'm sure that's not true," Avery said.

She blinked.

"I'm sure he made friends. I'm sure there are hundreds of people who will remember him, and always will," Avery continued, with more sincerity than I'd ever heard from him. "Was he funny?"

"Yeah." Kitty sniffed, wiping her eyes on the back of her wrist. "How'd you know?"

"Lucky guess. But anyway, I reckon fifty years from now, when all those soldiers are home with their grandkids, they'll keep telling stories about your brother and how he made them smile in one of the worst places in the world. I doubt they think he made no difference to them."

I saw Madon turn his head towards us with something like surprise. Kitty and I stared with equal disbelief, until Kitty launched herself forwards and threw her arms around Avery's neck. He stumbled backwards.

"You really reckon?" she mumbled into his shoulder.

"Sure." Avery mimicked the awkward pat on the back I'd given her. "You don't have to drop the biggest bomb to be a hero, after all."

"Hero." Kitty sniffed again and nodded. Realizing she'd dropped the telegram, she bent and picked it up, running her thumb along the creases. I kept watching Avery, expecting him to give me a wink or roll his eyes, but he kept himself perfectly serious. Oddly enough, he wasn't acting. "Who *are* you?"

"Avery...Sadler."

"Huh." She turned to me. "So you're properly back, eh?"

No. I'm here for as long as it takes me to figure out where Andrew is.

What could I say? Given the news, how could I bring up Andrew's disappearance without distressing her even further?

"Kitty," Avery said, quite gently. "Is Andrew about? We just need to talk to him."

Her thumb picked up its pace. "No. He ain't here no more."

"But he was?" Avery pushed. "Not too long ago?"

"I saw 'im yesterday. Least, I thought I did, but Aunt Jule tells me I'm imagining things 'cause of...of Billy. So I dunno."

"Was he alone?"

"No. Some girl was with 'im, I think she left when he did. Typical Andrew, ain't it?" She snorted, but there was no mirth behind the gesture. "Nothin' like you, Evelyn. Shortish. Weird hair, like it'd been straight-ironed. Nice dress, though, and a pretty shawl. You know her?"

"Oh, yes." I glanced at Avery. "We know her."

"What about a boy?" Madon interjected, dropping his sentry post. "Was there not another boy with them?"

"I was gettin' to that." Kitty frowned. "Aren't you the surveyor?"

"Was there a boy?" he repeated, harsher.

I didn't need to hear her answer. The boy in question stood perhaps ten yards away, dressed in nothing but grimy workers' overalls and a tatty shirt, with a pistol levelled directly between Kitty's shoulder blades. Catching my eye, he smiled and raised a finger to his lips.

"I *think* I saw someone else," Kitty was saying. "But like I said, I been muddled. He looked kinda like the girl, but...nicer. She scared me. I dunno what Andrew was doin' with her. They were gone again 'fore I could talk to 'im. What're you all starin' at?"

"Nothing, nothing," I said, taking her hand before she could turn around. "Um, do you know where they went? Did Andrew seem all right?"

Deio didn't lower the pistol. I tried to ignore him, to focus on Kitty, but this was far easier said than done. Madon didn't seem sure how to react, and Avery, like me, was steadfastly snubbing him.

"I think I heard 'em mention London. But they both seemed kinda worked-up. You sure there ain't nothin' behind me?"

"Quite, quite sure."

Deio made a gesture with the weapon, and behind me, Madon made a show of proving he was unarmed. I heard a *click*.

"Why don't you two take Miss Rogers inside?" Madon suggested.

"If any of you move," Deio countered, still smiling, "I'll fire all six of these bullets into her heart."

Chapter Twenty-Two

Kitty gave a cry of alarm, wrenching away from me and spinning around. She screamed again when she saw the gun. "That's him! That's—"

"You're the only dispensable person here, Miss Rogers, so if you value your life at all, you'll not say another word," Deio said politely.

"What do you want?" Avery asked with some of the deadpan insolence he used to aim at Tressa.

Deio exhaled, shoving one hand into his pocket and continuing to level the pistol with the other. "Isn't that just the question? I'll admit, you've really thrown a wrench this time, Avery."

"Thanks. It's my speciality."

Kitty squeaked, covering her mouth.

"And you—" Deio glanced at Madon— "you, just can't seem to choose which side you're on. Blood oath or no blood oath, Demitra will kill you when she realizes you risked everything to save *him*. If you were going to do it, why not take Penny?"

"It's always about bloody Penny," Avery muttered.

"I've watched them far more closely than you," Madon hissed. "I know what I'm doing."

"That's what I'm afraid of." Deio took a step forward, shifting his gaze back to Kitty. "Pity about your brother, by the way. My condolences."

His finger tightened around the trigger.

"Where's Andrew?" I said, moving directly in front of Kitty. "Why did you leave?"

"Ah, you're so clueless that it's almost endearing."

Again he was mocking! Having proven to myself what I was capable of back at the flat, it was all too tempting to gather the Others and show Deio that he wasn't toying with a helpless child anymore. As it was, I could only use my confidence to persuade him not to shoot me.

"Please move, Evelyn." His smile hardened. "Miss Rogers has seen and heard a tiny little bit too much."

"I won't tell no one anythin'," Kitty whispered. "Promise."

"I believe you." The wind tugged at Deio's auburn hair, and for a moment, he looked like the friendly poster boys on the agricultural recruitment posters. "But as I heard you say, one more death, one less—it doesn't matter either way."

"If you do it," I blurted, "you'll have nothing left to bargain with."

The pistol lowered, almost imperceptibly. "You're willing to bargain?"

"You're playing right into his hand," Madon hissed from behind me, unable to keep the desperation from his voice. "Don't be an idiot, girl."

"I am *not* an idiot!" I shouted, loudly enough that Madon fell silent, and Avery and Kitty flicked me identical glances of alarm. Taking a deep breath, I repeated, "I'm not an idiot and neither are any of you. So please, let Kitty go, and we can talk like sane people. If you do this—and tell me where Andrew is—then Avery and I will go with you to Boundary, no more questions asked, and we can finish this once and for all."

I was tired of waiting. I was starving, sleep-deprived, and finished with watching Madon and the Farthing twins taunt me with half-truths and promises wrapped around lies. I no longer cared about what ulterior motives Deio and Demitra had surrounding the fall of Boundary, and now Madon had made his position clear, they were once again my only option.

"Evelyn," Madon warned.

Deio moved the pistol across to Madon and gave a short laugh. "All right. It's your lucky day, Miss Rogers. Let's hope we don't meet again."

Without a word, Kitty turned tail and ran towards the farmyard, her red headscarf fluttering to the ground in her wake. Although my heart ached to run after her, I steeled myself and faced Deio.

"Where is Andrew?"

Deio paused for a moment before tucking the pistol inside his jacket. "London."

"London?"

"Yes." His smile widened. "Don't worry. Demitra is with him."

That, of course, was far from comforting.

"Why? Is he okay? What are you—?"

"I said I'd tell you where he was," Deio interrupted, "and I have. Shall we get going?"

He began walking out into the fields, hands in his pockets, heading for the distant hedge-lined horizon. Avery and I locked eyes in mutual agreement and had started to follow when a hand reached out and seized my upper arm.

"You'll kill them," Madon said. I could feel him shaking. "It's too late. The Boundary is far too unstable, and if you try to take it down, it will collapse and kill them."

"That's your own damn fault for taking Avery, isn't it?" Deio called, not turning around. "Come on, you two, keep up."

"They only want to save Penny. They'll let the others die. Better your friends are alive and trapped than dead."

"Debateable," Avery muttered.

I shook away from Madon's grasp. I'd never seen him look so panicked before; not when Penny activated the trials too early, not when the Farthing twins began intervening, not when Penny revealed she could Rip, and not even when I'd used the Others against him mere hours ago. He'd been relying on his ability to stop us, but he had forgotten one crucial detail: Harriet. Harriet, whether she knew it or not, was like me, and the Others felt it, massing around the farm just as they did in the Gloucester flat. He was powerless here.

"I will stop you," Madon called furiously to our retreating backs. "I *will*."

"He won't," said Deio.

I just focussed on my feet stumbling over the uneven ground and tried to forget the words,

'*You'll kill them.*'

* * *

We stopped in a copse of naked trees on the edge of the Pearson farm, out of sight of the road. Snow had started to fall from the stark grey sky, catching and melting in my eyelashes until it felt like I was crying. By now, I barely felt the cold.

"This should be far enough away," Deio remarked. "Although you're a better judge of that than I am. Are there many Others about?'

I cast out a mental net, then shook my head.

"Good." To my surprise, Deio reached into his jacket and handed Avery the pistol. "Just in case. Unfortunately, it's quite likely Madon will try to interfere at some point, and I'm under a blood oath not to harm him."

Avery turned the pistol over in his hand, clearly surprised too. "I don't even know how these work."

"Point and pull the trigger," Deio said. "I trust you'll use it as necessary."

Avery's jaw set as he nodded, and I knew that he wasn't lying. There was a reason why Deio had asked him over me.

"Now that's taken care of, we should get going. It's impossible to Rip anywhere without weakening the barrier, but..." Deio smiled his wide, dark smile. "We can't afford to let Madon beat us there."

So for the second time that day, I closed my eyes to the nausea and reopened them somewhere else.

And that somewhere else was the woods of Boundary.

Head spinning, it took me a moment to focus on my surroundings. A layer of snow covered the ground, and ice hung from the black trees like decorative crystals, where nothing moved except for a single crow perched overhead. It felt like I'd stepped into a twisted monochrome photo.

"I *hate* that sensation," Avery grumbled, hauling himself to his feet from where he'd fallen.

"If it were comfortable, everyone would do it," Deio said lightly. "Now, we're a good mile out—else we would've dragged far too many Others with us—so we'll have to go for a little hike."

There were no paths this deep within the woods, but winter had culled any undergrowth that might have made walking difficult. Aside from occasional thickets of dead brambles and hidden ditches blocking our way, we made quick progress. Avery and I hung a few paces back from Deio. I realized that I hadn't asked his input on whether or not we were doing the right thing, though I supposed now was too late to ask; besides, Avery wasn't the sort to go along with a plan he didn't agree with. So instead, I brought up the other issue that was bothering me.

"Do you think Andrew is all right?"

Avery shrugged. "I've never met him or Demitra. Who would you put your money on?"

"That's not what I'm saying," I said, stung by the flippancy of his tone. "I meant…I could've bartered harder to find out what they've done with him. But I didn't, and I worry…"

I worried because I'd proven to myself that I was willing to sacrifice him, if only for a time, to get closer to my friends. I worried because I was someone notorious for being sweet and innocent, yet there was a clear hierarchy in my head concerning who I'd let live and die if it ever came down to it. Andrew had abandoned his family for me. I had abandoned Andrew for mine.

"Don't worry," Avery said. "We've been over this. They'd gain nothing by hurting him."

"He knows what they are. He knows far more than Kitty, and

look what nearly happened to her."

"Fred and Andrew are both about to fall off a cliff. You can only save one. Who do you save?" Avery asked, sounding almost bored.

"Fred," I said automatically. "But that's a horrible, horrible question, and I don't see what that has to do with anything."

He raised an eyebrow. "Really?"

"Why can't I save both of them? Why is there no other option?"

"That's it, right there." Avery flashed a faint grin, pushing my side as if we were ten again. "You said you'd save Fred before you even asked if there was another option. Savage, eh?" My face must've betrayed my dismay, because the grin faded into something softer and he said, "Don't worry, Evelyn. Focus on what we're doing now."

Right. Bringing down Boundary. In a matter of hours, I could be with Fred, Penny, Tressa and Lucas again...

I bumped into the side of a tree and sent a cloud of snow spinning into the air. Deio stopped and turned around.

"I can hear you two talking, by the way."

"Good," I shot back.

"Speaking like that, I wonder if you could almost understand why we've done what we've done." Deio began walking again, almost sauntering. "Of course, trying to justify—"

He broke off.

I stared, wondering if he'd seen something. Madon, maybe? But the woods remained silent and still.

Avery frowned. "Deio?"

Nothing. It was as though he'd been frozen solid.

I walked up to him tentatively. "Are you...okay?" *Not that I care.*

Deio gave a strangled gasp and stumbled, leaning into a nearby tree. The Cheshire Cat smile had vanished, replaced with the sort of twisted grimace I'd seen on Andrew whenever his leg began acting up.

"Are you hurt?" Avery demanded.

"I don't *get* hurt," Deio spat from between clenched teeth. Then he doubled over with another gasp.

"Right, well, whenever you've finished not being hurt, can we keep moving?"

I hovered, unsure of what to do. There was no blood, he hadn't fallen, and no one else was around. Yet Deio never showed emotion, not aside from his false politeness, and it was clear the pain contorting his face was perhaps the first real thing he'd ever let us see.

"Deio, what's happening?"

"Burning," he choked. He'd gone white. "I...I feel...this shouldn't be..."

Deio's eyes squeezed shut, his breathing becoming more and more ragged. *I feel.* He'd said those two words with such terror that if it had been anyone else, I would've felt sorry for him. Despite it all, I almost did.

"What can we do?" I asked, crouching down and trying to ignore the snow seeping through my shoes. "You have to tell us what's wrong."

"We've got to..." Deio took a deep, shuddering breath and staggered to his feet. "We've got to keep going. Whatever's happening, we...we can't let it stop us."

"That's all fine and dandy, mate," Avery said, "but you look like death."

"Madon's not around?"

"No," I said, after scanning the bare woods. "No, it's just us."

"Someone is attacking me." Little by little, Deio's cool mask returned, although his skin retained a sickly pallor and I could see the pain flashing behind his eyes. "I don't know how. This shouldn't happen—not to me."

But I hadn't been lying; there was no one around. I could feel the hum of the Others, growing thicker the closer we got to Boundary, but they weren't doing this. Even Madon couldn't hurt someone from so far away.

How could it be an attack?

Twenty-Three

After a short time, the pain seemed to fade. Deio straightened, fixed his jacket, and surveyed the woods for himself, irritation not enough to hide his confusion.

"Someone *must* be here," he growled, more to himself than to us.

"It couldn't have been a Rip," I said. "The Others didn't react."

Deio stared at me and I noticed he was still shaking. "They didn't?"

"Maybe it's you." Avery had already begun walking again. "Maybe you're sick."

Deio mouthed the word *impossible*.

"You're all right to keep going?" I asked awkwardly. I couldn't bring myself to be sympathetic, but the rational side of me knew that we couldn't do this with Deio suffering. He certainly didn't *look* all right.

"We can't let it stop us," he repeated. But when he made to follow Avery, all the languidness was gone from his stride; he moved like he hadn't walked in years.

I glanced up at a crow which had been hopping from branch-to-branch following us. It cawed once and flew off, sending another plume of snow shimmering into the air.

Boundary. We had to focus on Boundary.

Even though I'd never seen the forest cloaked in snow before, the atmosphere surrounding Boundary was strong enough that I'd have been able to pinpoint it blind. I could feel the Others here; feel the odd static pressure wrapped around the trees; feel the increased sense of delicacy, almost, like if we trod too heavily then more than the icicles would break.

"Here's the creek." Avery dug a little hole with his foot and exposed a thin vein of frozen water. "Home sweet home."

"Right." Deio glanced over his shoulder at our trail of

footprints, discomfort still evident, before returning to the creek. "Here's how it works. The barrier between our world and theirs is thinnest right here—above the water—and thanks to Madon and Penny, it's already nearly broken. It's easier to break from the outside, but it's also more dangerous because of the Others. You'll be able to feel them, Evelyn?"

I nodded. They were everywhere, just waiting.

"Your job will simply be to keep them away from us," he said. "Don't underestimate how important that is. I'll create a Rip in the barrier between our worlds, and Avery, you've got to stop Boundary from collapsing while they escape."

Avery stared. "How do I even do that?"

"You can Rip, can't you?"

"Barely."

Deio stared right back, frowning. "But...oh, no matter. Demitra will be here soon and she can take over, but until then, just try to reinforce the Rips I make."

"Reinforce," Avery echoed, sounding thoroughly unconvinced. "Right."

"I should also add that there's a chance you might see things. Try to ignore them, all right?"

"See things?" Avery and I asked together.

Deio either ignored us or didn't hear. "As soon as we breach the barrier, Boundary won't be able to stand by itself anymore. Two worlds can't overlap for long. So know that if either of you break concentration, whoever is still left inside will be as good as dead."

Great, so now I have to risk my friends' lives too, I thought bitterly.

The worst part—Avery would agree with me—was the unknowing. We'd been discussing taking down Boundary for months, and now that we were here, I felt far too unprepared. There were more Others spread throughout this forest than the flat and the farm combined, and the implications of failing to hold them back were beyond terrifying. Avery hadn't been lying about his poor Ripping skills, and Deio still looked as if he was seconds away from keeling over. Then there was Andrew, and Madon's threat, and a thousand other worries clouding my mind—now Deio was suggesting hallucinations were also a possibility?

"Ready?" Deio asked.

I've been ready forever.

No.

Beside me, Avery gave an uncharacteristically nervous laugh.

Before I had time to ask one of the thousand questions burning inside my head, a Rip sliced through the silence of the forest. A heartbeat later, the Others came.

Two children sit on a bench, wearing matching outfits and matching expressions of fear. They both have auburn hair and dark eyes that make them almost indistinguishable. They can't be more than four years old. One of them reaches out and takes the other's hand.

"It's going to be okay. It always is."

"Ignore it!" Deio shouted.

"What was that?" Avery shouted back. "It was like I was standing somewhere else, I…"

"The Boundary is tied with the memories of those who created it." Deio had his hand outstretched in front of him, trying to control the monumental Rip he'd opened. "Releasing them… look, please just try to ignore it."

I couldn't reply. I was too busy mentally screaming at the Others to stay away, even though the sheer weight of them was nearly suffocating. To anyone watching, I wasn't facing anything more than an empty wood, lit with midmorning sun and glittering ice crystals. They wouldn't be able to see the invisible hoards that were straining towards Deio's Rip, held back only by a single thought.

The children are older, perhaps ten. Unmistakably Deio and Demitra. Surrounding them are about half a dozen adults. One, a younger woman with a disarming snaggletooth, approaches Deio and reaches out as though to embrace him. Instead, she drives a switchblade into his upper arm.

Deio stares at her. He doesn't flinch.

From behind them, a scream wrenches from Demitra's mouth. She drops to her knees and clutches her shoulder as though she was the one being stabbed.

"Interesting," the woman lisps. With a jerk, she twists the blade. Demitra's screams redouble.

"Why are you doing this?" Deio asks. "You're hurting her."

"Exactly." The woman twists the blade yet again. Her fist is covered with blood. "I'm hurting her.*"*

Hate flashes across Deio's expression, and he wrenches away, removing the knife and tossing it to the floor. Oblivious to his wound, he crouches beside a quivering Demitra and glares at the surrounding adults.

"You've tested this before. You know the answer. Leave us alone now."

The vision faded. I fought the urge to turn and see Deio's reaction, but knew that if I moved, if I tried to speak, I'd let the Others through. I couldn't see what progress they were making behind me. All I could do was close my eyes and focus on the imaginary shield I'd created, ignore the pressure coming at me from all sides, and ignore the battering of memories being thrown into my mind, a whirlwind of voices and flashed images. Every now and then, with the stronger memories, another scene would play out.

"Here comes a candle to light you to bed, and here comes a chopper to chop off your head," Demitra sings, twirling. "Chop, chop, chop."

With the final 'chop', she bends down and strikes something hidden behind a desk. Blood spatters across the wallpaper.

"Must you be so messy?" Deio asks.

Demitra stops dancing and stares at him with mania in her eyes. "Look at your hands."

Sure enough, his palms are stained crimson. He shrugs and wipes them on his trousers.

"They didn't deserve to have it done cleanly," she says, the singsong quality of her voice making it all the more unnerving. "We could've made it clean if we'd wanted to. But we didn't."

She bends down again, then faces the wall and begins to paint the word FARTHING in red letters. Then she freezes.

"Someone's still here."

Deio takes a fire poker, lying discarded on the floor, and nudges open a wardrobe.

A man hides there, terrified. It's a younger Madon.

Deio smiles at him and raises the poker.

"Wait," Madon blurts, hands raised. "Please. I can help you."

"Nobody can help us," Demitra says.

"I can."

Nausea wrenched through my stomach. Concentrate. I had to concentrate. The Others were becoming more and more relentless, more desperate. Our reality was destroying them. Perhaps they'd be able to thrive better inside Boundary. Perhaps that was why they were trying so hard to reach it.

I blinked away stars, surprised by how heavy my eyelids were becoming. I wanted to sleep forever.

Think of Fred. Think of Penny and Tressa and Lucas. Nothing else mattered.

Demitra stands in what looks like an abandoned industrial lot. She paces, chewing her lip, nervousness palpable. She holds a chubby toddler in her arms, but awkwardly—she's never held a child before. The toddler begins to grizzle.

Madon rushes into the scene, stopping dead when he sees her.

"Where is the child from? What have you done?" he demands. "Where is Deio?"

Demitra shakes her head, tears beginning to slide down her cheeks. "He's cleaning up. He'll be here soon."

"Cleaning up what?"

She's crying now. The toddler starts wailing in earnest.

"Demitra, answer me," Madon says roughly. "What did you do?"

"My sister. This is my sister." Demitra kisses the carroty fuzz atop the toddler's head, tightening her grip. "I—I didn't mean to... my parents didn't recognize me, and they...they were afraid of me. I thought they might still love me, but they didn't, and I...I lost control."

If this surprises Madon in any way, he doesn't show it.

"I thought your parents were dead."

"So did I." Demitra sniffs. "Turns out I can't trust my own memories. Oh, well. They're certainly dead now."

"That's impossible!" Avery shouted. "These can't be real!"

"Concentrate," Deio snarled back. "Evelyn, you're letting them through."

Of course I was letting them through. It was like trying to keep water in a bucket full of holes; no matter how hard I tried to cover everywhere, the Others leaked through. There were too many of them. And, try as I might, I couldn't help but dwell on the memories flashing in and out of my head. Like Avery said, the timeline didn't match up, yet the emotions were so strong...

They're outside Boundary now, almost exactly where we are standing. Demitra, Deio, Madon, infant Penny—and Beatrix.

"You're sure this will work?" Madon asks.

"Don't you trust me?" Deio gives a lazy laugh. "There's another world, a vacant world, right here. I can feel it."

"We don't know if it's stable."

"It will be." Deio says it with utter confidence.

Demitra is staring at Beatrix, who holds Penny in her arms. Beatrix's face is knitted with a tender love; Penny is fast asleep, dreaming.

"You'll take care of her," Demitra says. It's not a question.

"Like she was my own." Beatrix glances at Madon with something like sadness, before returning to Penny. "Although the poor darling will be rather lonely if you keep her in there forever."

"Not forever," Deio says, though he sounds like he couldn't care less. "Until it's safe."

Demitra, however, seems worried. "Lonely? But you said you'd be there, always."

"I'm old, my dear. How much company can I give a child?"

Demitra nods. An odd look comes over her. "No one should be alone," she whispers.

My heart began pounding. I was beginning to understand where the story was heading, and I didn't like it.

"Evelyn!" Deio shouted. "Damn it, focus on the Others!"

The entire reason behind our captivity was being revealed, and I could no more ignore it than I could stop breathing. Despite what I'd believed, this wasn't about our gifts at all. It had always been about Penny from the beginning.

"Evelyn, please!"

"I'm going to hide upstairs!" Penny laughs, her gown muddied and torn at the hem.

"You mustn't!" another girl whines. Her black hair is thick and glossy, her face full and bright, creased with displeasure.

I look so young. I barely recognize myself.

Demitra stands behind the cedar, watching us run away. Even when she steps on a twig and breaks it, neither of us seem to notice she's there.

"There you are." Deio materializes out of nowhere. "You've got to stay away, Demitra. This isn't helping anyone."

"She's our age now," Demitra whispers. "Soon she'll be older than us."

"We knew this would happen." Deio looks bored. "Time moves faster in the other layer just as it moves differently in all the layers. There's nothing we can do about it."

"Why can't we let them out? We could use her, we could—"

"Because she doesn't even know how to Rip yet," Deio snaps, and Demitra closes her mouth. "Because concentrating on this place is the only thing stopping Madon from interfering with our work. Because they're stuck in a pseudo-Victorian world thanks to your little eccentricity, and know nothing about the outside world, because you didn't want them to. And because there's a fairly serious war happening. Until she's mature enough to be tested—to discover her power—she's useless to us."

Demitra nods far too many times, like a bobble-headed doll. "He hurts them."

"He stops them from asking questions." Deio turns and walks through the forest. The trees appear to bend away from him, clearing his path.

Demitra hovers a moment longer, watching Penny and I find separate hiding places. Then she follows her brother and vanishes.

Focus. Focus.

Avery was saying—shouting—something to Deio. A humming in my ears blocked out the words, that scrambled fuzziness that usually comes seconds before passing out, where the world seems to be disappearing around you.

The Others were relentless. I was so, so tired. The visions came faster, more like blips, more of Madon arguing with the twins over controlling the world within Boundary, and Deio arguing with Demitra over her obsession with watching us, and Beatrix arguing with Madon over his use of torture, and Demitra arguing with Deio over setting Penny free. All the dark secrets that had been absorbed by the Boundary being thrown rapid-fire into the open. Then:

Madon stands over Beatrix's body, anguish tearing his face into something terrifying.

"How could you?" he roars when Deio and Demitra appear. "How could you?"

"She was telling them about the trials," Deio says. "I am sorry, but if she kept at it—"

"There are other ways to deal with people." The sudden calm in Madon's voice is more unsettling than the rage.

Deio only smiles his perfect, insincere smile. "The best part is that you have to admit to doing it. They're breaking your rules. They need some fear. Else they'll start seeing you for what you really are—weak."

No. No. No.

My blood turned to ice. These memories couldn't be true, they couldn't, they couldn't...Madon was cruel, tyrannical, and sadistic, but he wasn't half the monster I'd believed him to be. The real monster stood behind me yelling my name.

"Evelyn, look. We're doing it!"

Barely able to process his words, I twisted my head around. Boundary.

The manor, the lawns—albeit in a terrible state, but still there. And four figures in old-fashioned dress standing on the other side of the creek, growing more and more substantial by the second.

My eyes locked with Fred's. He mouthed my name, but I couldn't hear him. Despite my tears, I laughed a hoarse, gasping laugh.

"We're doing it!"

Stay away, stay away, stay away. My shield became a chant, growing stronger and stronger.

"You've got to cross the creek," Deio shouted. "Penny, do it now!"

Penny hesitated. She took a step forward.
Then a Rip tore through the forest.
No! Don't let it collapse!
The chant broke and the shield dissipated.
Boundary vanished.

Chapter Twenty-Four

Avery swore, stumbling backwards and nearly knocking me over. *Did you see what I saw?* He didn't need to say the words for me to know what his expression meant.

Deio, on the other hand, stood rigid by the creek. An incalculable rage was beginning to dance behind the deathlike sheen that still clung to his face, and I automatically took a step away.

"Who's there," he said, toneless. Then he wrenched around and screamed, "Who's there? Madon!"

Madon dragged himself out from behind a copse of trees, seeming horridly satisfied. "I did warn you."

"You've destroyed it." Deio's tone grew cold again. "It's gone. *They're* gone. All those years…and you've…what were you thinking?"

"I realized that it was going to fall anyway." Madon shrugged. "So you ask me why I destroyed it? Spite. You don't always get to win, Deio. You've been winning for far too long without consequence—nothing more than a child who hasn't ever faced discipline…yet."

Spite. I might never see Fred again because all my friends and I had ever been to them were counters in a game that never should have involved us. Only this game wasn't black and white, good and bad; both sides were just as vindictive and wicked as the other, and innocent people were dying in the crossfire.

"You killed Beatrix," I said, whirling on Deio. "And our parents."

"And many, many others." Deio waved his hand, still fixated on Madon with a burning fury. "None of that matters now."

"You kept us under a bell jar. You took away everything from us for your own gain. Don't you see?" I blinked away my tears. They were freezing on my cheeks, numbing my skin. "You're exactly like those people who tortured *you.*"

"Evelyn's right," Avery said flatly. "You're..."

He didn't seem to be able to find a strong enough word.

I couldn't think. Nothing felt real anymore. I didn't know what to do, what else to say...so I just watched Madon and Deio with a heart of ice.

"You look ill," Madon was saying.

"Breaking into Boundary took effort." Deio spat each syllable.

"Are you angry with me?"

"Of course I'm—"

A change came over him. The fury faded away and was replaced by something else, an expression I'd never seen Deio wear before: fear.

"For Evelyn and Avery's benefit," Madon said, flicking us a glance, "should I tell them a little story about you and Demitra?"

I thought of the twisting knife and shuddered.

Madon, however, appeared to be enjoying himself. "That's what made the pair of them so valuable. Demitra absorbed all his emotion, all his pain—imagine, an assassin without a conscience who couldn't be hurt, and a counterpart so mentally overwhelmed that she lost her humanity too. A psychopath and a lunatic."

"Stop," Deio warned.

"Yet," Madon went on, moving ever closer, "you say you're angry with me? You, Deio?"

I wanted to point out that I didn't care about Deio's feelings—or lack thereof—at that moment. I didn't care why the twins were 'valuable', and I didn't care if Madon felt a lesson needed to be taught. I clung to a hope that somehow Boundary had survived the Rip, meaning that every precious moment spent bickering was a moment that we should be using to free my friends... but no sooner was I about to say all this aloud, I was cut off by another figure emerging from behind the trees.

I must've been dreaming after all.

Andrew.

Here.

"Andrew," I cried. I was about to run over and throw my arms around him, but something in his expression stopped me.

There was something very, very wrong about this.

"Where is Demitra?" Deio demanded.

Madon stared at him. "Time for another story, I think."

Andrew avoided my gaze. "I don't think we need to go there. He knows."

"They don't." Madon nodded at us.

A thousand tiny cuts were scattered across Andrew's face as if he'd run through brambles, and he stood with his shoulders slumped. The kindness and cheer I'd grown used to was gone— he just looked exhausted.

"I didn't tell you the whole truth about the car accident," Andrew began, almost whispering. "It wasn't an accident at all, you see."

A vein in Deio's temple began to tick.

"We were about half a mile from home when this car came hurtling down the lane...far too fast, and it..." Andrew squeezed his eyes closed. "It ploughed her over like she wasn't there. There was nothing I could've done afterwards, she...her neck..." He trailed off again. "I ran after the car and it ended up stopping. The driver was just a kid, just another teenager. Claimed it was a mistake. But I was so upset, I kept screaming at him over and over and over and I swear, all he did was *look* at my leg, and..."

"Let me guess," Avery said, "it was Deio."

Andrew nodded. I willed him to look at me, to give me some reassurance that everything would be all right, but he continued to stare at the snow-covered ground.

"The doctor said that I'd been hit by the car too. That I'd been delirious. The whole thing was written off as an accident, and I'd nearly started believing it when *he* turned up at the farm talking to Evelyn. And Evelyn told me about Boundary and the existence of magic and I realized...I realized I hadn't been delirious. Beth hadn't been going mad."

"Is that why you came with me?" I asked, aghast. "Not because you wanted to help?"

"I wanted answers."

Madon gave a little laugh. "You didn't think that he accepted your story a little hastily, Evelyn?"

Andrew ignored him, and me, continuing, "Then we found that diary. They were killing people with powers—that's why they got Beth. And all I could think of was Harriet."

Piece by piece, everything fell into place. Ours was a story crowned by revenge cycles, and Andrew had simply become another Bella Whatley.

"That's why you left the flat?" I asked Deio. "He threatened to expose you?"

"Yes," Deio scorned. "Pearson, like so many others, threatened to kill us, too. We'd been recognized far too many times in the West Country already, so we decided to move northwards— after dealing with him first. As if *he* could kill *us!*"

"But you didn't deal with him." Andrew confronting them must have forced them to vacate the flat early. And of course they couldn't disappear north without first finishing their goal getting Penny out of Boundary. What happened though between Deio, Demitra and Andrew I couldn't work out.

Deio saw my frown and continued. "I went to the farm and waited for you in case you went straight there, Demitra stayed to 'deal' with Andrew as we knew he would come looking for you. Though she doesn't appear to have done that very well."

"She found me when you went after *him*," said Andrew, glancing at Avery. "I knew then I'd made a mistake. She couldn't be reasoned with, and she was going to...well, I probably wouldn't have escaped in one piece. So I bargained. I remembered what you said about them tracking down gifted people, and I said I knew of someone who could Rip in London. A life for a life, right? I have relatives in London, and I thought if

I could just get away, if I could lose her and I'd be able to lay low until…" He shook his head, looking somewhat dazed. "She took the bait. We went to the farm first to speak with Deio to tell him what we were doing. He agreed saying it wouldn't hurt to have a someone else who could Rip. Then we went to London. But we only just arrived when the air raid sirens started going off."

The little colour remaining in Deio's skin vanished. A flash of something like grief passed over his face, and for a moment I thought he might cry. Then he darkened.

"You saved him, didn't you?" Deio whispered to Madon. "You saved him, and you left her there to die."

"She was already going to die." Madon said each word with relish. "She got crushed by a beam when the building collapsed."

"So it's your fault." Deio turned to Andrew.

My nails bit into the palms of my hands, the gravity of the situation becoming clearer and clearer. Demitra was dead. Numb from the speed of the events of these past few hours, I quite honestly didn't know how to feel. Upset? Relieved? Nothing at all?

"Madon told me all about you," Andrew said, "how you've never felt remorse for a single thing you've done. So you know what? Maybe I never had it in me to do the job myself, but I'm glad your sister died in that air raid. I'm glad you're finally going to learn what it means to suffer."

"You think we made you suffer?" Deio cocked his head. "Not even close."

I saw Deio move out of the corner of my eye, too fast for me to register what he was doing until it was too late. Another Rip shattered the peacefulness of the woods, and after a second, Andrew began screaming. The pressure of the Others built up again.

"Stop!" I cried. "Deio, stop!"

Deio, of course, did nothing of the sort. He looked as if he was trying to maintain his characteristic coolness, but it was gradually being swallowed by a terror—terror, I supposed, of terror itself.

Andrew writhed in the snow, screams becoming silent. Madon watched and did nothing.

"You can't Rip here!" Not knowing what else to do, I grabbed Deio's arm. "There are too many Others already, you'll ruin Boundary for good."

"It's already ruined," Deio snarled.

But as the pressure increased, a nearby tree fell with an ear-splitting creak and Deio let the Rip dissipate. Avery rushed over to Andrew's side.

"He's all right. He just—"

Andrew grabbed at something and stumbled to his feet. He'd taken the pistol from Avery's pocket.

"I should shoot you. I'd probably be saving lives by doing it."

Remarkably calmly, Avery shifted position so that he stood directly in the pistol's line of fire. "Can't let you do that yet, my friend. We've got some unfinished business."

Andrew stared. "Who the hell even *are* you?"

"Someone who really, really doesn't have time for this vendetta rubbish at the moment. Tomorrow? Blow his heart out for all I care. Right now? Back off."

How surreal it all was. Andrew pointing a lethal weapon at Avery, who was trying to protect Deio, who looked lost in his own mind, while Madon and I hung back trying to decide whether or not to intervene. The Others continued to circle, and behind me I still felt the strange presence of Boundary—I refused to believe it had collapsed. Not entirely.

"Get out of my way," Andrew ordered quietly. "Or I swear to God I'll shoot you too."

"You're not like this, Andrew," I said, chilled by the resignation in his tone. "Please put the gun down."

For the first time, Andrew raised his eyes and looked at me. "I wanted to help your friends, you know. Even if they blinded you from seeing anything else properly. Don't you care about Harriet? About me?"

"Harriet Pearson is no threat." Deio gave a single, sharp shake of his head. "If you'd done your research, you'd know that only people who can Rip are targets, since—"

"Shut up!" Andrew shoved Avery out of the way and levelled the pistol at the centre of Deio's chest. "You stole Beth, you stole my chance to serve with my brothers—you stole my *life*."

"What, you didn't think I spared you that night out of mercy?" Deio scorned. "It's the far crueller punishment to be left the survivor in those situations. If I'd wanted you to have a good life, I'd—"

"Shut up!"

A shot rang out. Birds took to the skies, shrieking their surprise. Deio's hand flew to his shoulder where the bullet grazed him, leaving a trail of blood in its wake.

"No, damn it!" Avery barrelled into Andrew just as he fired again, sending the second bullet racing into the leafless canopy. Andrew turned and hit Avery over the head with the barrel of the pistol, almost causing him to lose his footing, but Avery wasn't the type to back down from a fight easily. Though Andrew was both physically larger and armed, Avery had got into enough scraps within Boundary to know how the game was played. His fist made contact with Andrew's jaw and the pistol clattered to the ground.

"Aren't you going to do something?" I spun around to face Deio.

Deio's fingers flickered over the graze. "It's too late. Just make sure you tell Pearson that I'll be coming for him."

He took off running, and without thinking twice, I ran after him.

Chapter Twenty-Five

"Evelyn." Madon stepped out in front of me, blocking my way.

"Let me through!"

"He couldn't save Boundary if he wanted to, not in his state. After the shock has worn off, well—" Madon's lips twitched into a cold smile— "he won't have the focus to Rip for a while."

"What's it to you?" I hissed, biting down a rising panic.

Madon flicked a careless glance across the woods, where Avery had Andrew in a headlock and was shouting obscenities at him. Then his black eyes focussed on me again. "Nothing. Nothing at all. Though I suppose I've distracted you long enough now—you won't catch Deio. It's over."

It's over.

Something inside me buckled.

Madon tipped his hat and melted away into the copse of trees, heading in the opposite direction to Deio.

"Wait," Andrew called. "You promised me...protection..."

"You failed," Madon shouted, as he passed out of view. "I really thought you might've been strong enough to finish both of them off."

Then he was gone.

Avery dropped Andrew, cursing even more colourfully. "That's it? They're both running away?"

I stared at the empty expanse of woodland surrounding us, willing Deio to reappear. Or Demitra, with her mad little laugh, insisting the whole charade had been an elaborate joke. It wasn't over. It couldn't be over.

"I'm sorry, Evelyn." Andrew didn't try to get up, his face buried in his hands. "I didn't mean for things to end up like this."

"You need to get out of here," I said to Andrew through a growing lump in my throat. "You need to go somewhere far away and you need to hide. You don't have any abilities for him to track, so you have a chance."

Andrew jerked his head. "He'll find me. I-I...I never meant..."

I wondered if perhaps I should comfort him, but in all honesty, he hadn't told me the whole truth. He'd hidden things from me. As Madon pointed out, he'd believed my story a little too quickly and I should have guessed. Besides, it wasn't as if Andrew had *murdered* Demitra, not like she'd murdered Beth and Beatrix and all those others, and I couldn't fault him for wanting revenge, for wanting his family to be safe again.

But I'd lost Boundary because of him.

I turned my back on Andrew, feeling cold inside.

Avery, a bruise swelling underneath his right eye, followed me with a similar deadened expression. "We can still try. Maybe we're better off without Deio anyway."

"Neither of us know what we're doing." I stared out over the creek, remembering how vivid Fred's form had been—almost as if I could have touched him. "Besides, it takes three, remember? And after that Rip, there are far too many Others around for—"

I broke off, an idea dawning.

Others. Plural.

"Evelyn?" Avery nudged my arm.

What had been the last command I gave?

Don't let it collapse.

It was so simple, all this time, all this worrying about finding a team of three, and I'd had access to hundreds the entire time. Demitra and Deio had told me to keep the Others at bay to hide the alternative—the Others themselves could be used to stop Boundary from falling apart. All we needed was someone to control the Others and someone to open the barrier, meaning Avery and I were enough without them.

"Do you see the Rip Deio made between the barriers?" I asked, whirling on Avery. "Is it still there?"

Avery gave me a look, but squinted at the empty air above the creek just the same. His eyebrows flew up.

"Right there." He pointed at something I couldn't see. "It's faint, practically invisible. But why didn't it close? Neither of us were maintaining it."

I didn't answer, my head reeling. If Avery forced it open again, opened the barrier enough for our friends to run through, could the Others continue to stop Boundary from collapsing? Or would they grow destructive again as soon as I tried switching commands? What about the Others drawn here by Deio and Madon's Rips? Could I control two groups at once?

Did we have another choice?

"Open it."

"What?" He blinked. It was satisfying to see him genuinely confused. "That won't do anything but make more of a mess."

"Trust me," I said, wishing I felt as confident as I sounded. Although, it wasn't as if we had anything to lose.

Avery seemed to reach the same conclusion. He glanced at Andrew—even now, he wouldn't miss an opportunity to show off—and, a heartbeat later, the woods were once again filled with the humming pressure of the Others.

Don't let it collapse. Don't let it collapse. Don't let it collapse.

Over and over and over again. More memories and visions kept flashing through my mind, but this time, even they couldn't distract me. The Farthings and Madon weren't going to lose me my friends again.

Don't let it collapse. Don't let it collapse. Don't let it collapse.

Whether it was working or not, I couldn't tell. Vaguely, I heard Avery speaking. But all my concentration was used up, all my energy devoted to a single chant.

Don't let it collapse. Don't let it collapse. Don't let it collapse.

"Evelyn, stop! You've got to stop!"

I scrunched my eyes closed as blackness threatened to swallow my vision.

"Evelyn! Listen to me!"

I couldn't listen. I couldn't break concentration. I couldn't lose them.

Don't let it collapse. Don't let it collapse. Don't let it collapse.

I felt Avery tugging at my arm, but I shook him off.

"Evelyn!"

My eyes flew open. For a moment, all I saw was a kaleidoscope of dancing stars.

Then I saw *her*.

Chapter Twenty-Six

"Penny?" I gasped.

She didn't answer, but threw her arms around my shoulders in a typically suffocating hug. She'd grown taller, her red hair now below her chin in a way that reminded me far too much of her sister. Still, when she broke away, she was grinning in a contagious manner that I'd never seen Demitra mirror, and the flicker of apprehension passed.

"You're here," I managed to say, knees buckling. "You're really here."

"Present and accounted for. But cripes, Evelyn, you look... well, awful. What are you *wearing*?"

"You two sound as if you've swapped places," Lucas noted wryly. He hadn't changed a bit, his limbs still too long for the rest of his body, his eyes still their piercing violet-blue. "Although she has a point. What *are* you wearing?"

The curiosity with which he'd spoken hadn't changed either, then.

Bit by bit, my exhaustion seeped away and I saw them properly. One, two, three, four—all of them. They were all here.

I'd done it.

Penny, bouncing on her heels with her uncontainable energy; Lucas, continuing to frown at my clothes; Tressa, sharp features pulled into an uncharacteristic grin, white blonde hair seeming to blend with the snow; and there, next to her, was Fred.

A muffled sob escaped me. Before I'd registered anything else, the five of us were piled together in a tight embrace, and if only for a heartbeat, it felt as if nothing had changed at all since I'd seen them last. Even though we'd been worlds apart, in that moment, none of it mattered.

"Avery," I said, realizing he was missing. I twisted around and saw him hovering a few steps away.

I felt Penny tense.

Avery raised his palms to the air. "I swear, I only —"

"We were going to take the Boundary down ourselves," she said, her smile dropping into a scowl. "We could've done it. You abandoned us, Avery."

"Abandoned? That's a little harsh."

"Why, what would you call it?"

"Without him," I interjected, "you wouldn't be here right now. He actually...he..." Another bought of dizziness overtook me and I wobbled to the ground. My heart drowned out the feelings of sickness, singing, *They're here! They're here!* with a happiness I hadn't experienced in far, far too long. We hadn't even needed Deio in the end. We were, all of us, free.

"You've got no idea how long we've been waiting for this," Tressa said, bending down and squeezing my hand.

"Nearly as long as I have?"

"You need to tell us *everything.*" Penny paced around the woods, eyes dancing, running her fingers over the bark and snow and icicles like she'd been dropped into Wonderland.

"Everything?" I said. *Your sister is dead. You unleashed demonic forces trying to escape Boundary. If this war keeps going, we'll lose the boys. Madon didn't kill Beatrix. I'm far more powerful than you think I am. Your brother is a murderer. And Boundary was created—we were trapped—because of you.* I cracked a smile. "Definitely."

"Start with telling me who that is, maybe."

Penny pointed at Andrew, who'd flattened himself in the shadows of a large tree. I realized that he'd seen the full extent of mine and Avery's abilities, and wondered if he thought I was a monster now too. His cheekbone sported a colourful bruise from Avery's punch, and his mouth hung open.

"This is Andrew," I said. Then, to Andrew, "I thought I told you to run?"

"I..."

"Run from what?" Lucas asked.

"Not what," Avery corrected, flashing Andrew a cold grin.

"Who."

"All right, who then?"

"Nobody." I glared at Avery, jerking my head in Penny's direction. I didn't want to ruin the moment by explaining every dark truth we'd uncovered about Boundary. Not here. Not until we'd figured out where we were going to stay, or how we were going to explain four—five, if we counted Avery—teenagers in old-fashioned clothing and no official past to the authorities. We couldn't go to Julia, not without Andrew, and I had no doubt that Deio would try to contact Penny eventually...

"Don't I get a personal hello?" Fred nudged me, tone only half-joking. "I mean, it has been a while, but—"

I cut him off with a hug, burying my face in his shoulder. Everything about him felt like home and I never wanted to let go, never, ever again...

"You're crying," he said, gently.

"I always cry." I wiped my eyes, pulling away and drinking him in. "You know that."

"Over torn hems and petty insults," he teased. "You just... you seem to be properly crying this time."

"I'm *happy*, Fred."

Right in the edge of my vision, I saw Andrew limping away into the forest. Should I have called him back? Offered protection? Simply said goodbye?

The answer to that, of course, would come later.

But then and there, letting him go seemed to be the only thing to do.

I watched my friends as though in a dream, watched them observing the world with wide smiles and the amazement of being able to walk however far they wanted. Little by little though, fear replaced my elation, gnawing at my nerves in its typical insidious way. I thought of the recruitment posters plastered across the city walls, the gasmasks and air raids that Demitra had proved could touch even us. The bleakness of the countryside, the hunger, the constant need to use less and less and less and Kitty's anguish over her brother, mere years older than us, gunned down on some faraway continent.

How could I tell them that the real world wasn't so wonderful after all?

No. Thinking like that would get us nowhere. The alternative had been staying in a false reality, suffering at the whim of twisted people like Madon and the Farthings. Yes, things were dark and dangerous here too, but this offered us something Boundary never could: the ability to choose.

And so, sun catching the ice crystals and sending rainbows spinning between trees, I convinced myself to bury the fear. Tomorrow, we would figure everything out. We were once again six: Penny, Avery, Tressa, Lucas, Fred, and me.

Nothing, I vowed, would tear us apart again. Not if I had anything to do with it.

Epilogue

Avery walked through the village with his head down. He still fitted into that golden age category—too young to be frowned at for not enlisting, and too old to be frowned at for wandering about during a school day—and as a result, no one gave him a sideways glance. Of course, had anyone decided to take a closer look, they'd soon have noticed much to be suspicious about. The pockets of Avery's coat were stuffed with packets of crackers, tinned soup, and jars of pickled vegetables, yet he held no money. No money, no identification, no *anything*.

Well, except for an Enfield pistol.

Avery wasn't sure if it was loaded or not, though having examined it, he suspected only one bullet remained. He wasn't entirely sure how to use it, but he enjoyed the feeling of invincibility it brought. Even now, there was something unnerving about walking alone.

Alone.

He wondered how long it would take for that word to become less of a curse and more of a wish.

"Avery?"

His back went rigid in surprise. He debated ignoring the voice, but the sound of quickening footsteps made that impossible. The contents of his pockets meant running was impossible too, so steeling himself, Avery turned and faced the speaker.

"Andrew." His lips twitched into a smirk at the sight of a bruise blossoming under the other boy's eye. "It's been a while, eh?"

Andrew didn't look amused. "What're you doing here?"

"Sightseeing."

"Where did you get all that food?"

"What, this?" Avery glanced at the jars and cans in mock astonishment. "No idea."

Andrew's expression darkened. Glancing over his shoulder,

he grabbed Avery's upper arm and pulled him into a backstreet between two buildings. Avery shook him off, annoyed.

"What are you playing at?"

"Evelyn told me you were a pain in the arse," Andrew snapped. Then he seemed to get a hold of himself, and the anger ebbed away. "You've been stealing, haven't you?"

Avery regarded Andrew, considering whether it would be smart to flash the pistol. "Yeah. We're all starving."

"How did you ever get away with that?"

"Magic." Avery bared his teeth in a grin. "Distracting the clerks by toppling over every display at once also helps."

"You're going to drag them all into trouble."

Avery's grin vanished. "Says the one who killed Demitra bloody Farthing and nearly half my friends to boot."

The darkness returned, along with a flash of what was unmistakably guilt. "I didn't *mean* to kill her! It wasn't my fault that Madon chose not to save her, and it wasn't my fault that those bombs hit when they did. Raids usually don't happen in the daytime, and I thought...I thought by going to London I was..." He broke off, exhaling. "But done is done. I accept that."

"Good." Avery regarded him warily. "I'll leave you to it, then."

"You can tell Evelyn that I'll stay away. Whatever happens between Deio Farthing and me, I won't involve her."

Avery stared. What was he supposed to say to that? 'Thank you'? Clearly, Andrew had played a significant part in Evelyn's life before Avery broke out of Boundary, but all he'd brought to Avery was trouble.

But since the alternative was returning to the forest and enduring a mixture of Penny's still-simmering resentment and Evelyn's infuriatingly knowledgeable life lessons, Avery didn't move from the alley.

"You'll be all right, though?" Andrew asked awkwardly. "The group of you?"

Avery gestured to his full pockets. "We'll do the same as you, I suppose. Manage."

Andrew inclined his head, accepting this. "At least she seemed happy. Evelyn, I mean. With that Fred."

"Yes." Avery wrinkled his nose. "They'll be insufferable now. If he can tolerate new tough-girl Evelyn—and if she can tolerate him. Out of all of us, I think old Freddie changed the least."

"Isn't that a good thing?"

"I'm not sure yet." Stomach rumbling, Avery reached into his coat and withdrew the packet of crackers and opening it took one out. Through a full mouth, he added, "You really need to work on your fugitive skills, by the way. Running to the closest village and jumping out the second you see someone you recognize? That'll get you into trouble, my friend."

"I can't just 'magic' myself food." Andrew frowned at the main street behind them, as though only just realizing how exposed they were. "And I...I don't know where else to go. Madon promised to help me, but—"

Avery snorted. "Surprise, surprise, he didn't."

"No."

Perhaps that would change, Avery thought. To any of Deio's enemies, Andrew Pearson had become an incredibly useful weapon—someone who he not only blamed for the death of his sister, but was incapable of tracking the usual way, although, if he kept flaunting himself in public, the game wouldn't take long to be over.

"You've got an odd look," Andrew said uneasily. "What's on your mind?"

"I forgot to grab a can opener." Avery didn't skip a beat. "Oh, well. I better get going."

Something in Andrew's expression fell. "Right. Tell Evelyn..." He stumbled over his words for a moment, and then looked away. "Never mind."

When Andrew didn't move, Avery tucked everything out

of sight within his coat as best he could and strode out of the alley without looking back. He couldn't offer further help—he had enough to worry about without harbouring Deio Farthing's number one target.

Besides, Andrew had left his own bruises on Avery. And Avery Sadler wasn't the type to forgive quickly.

He'd nearly reached the edge of the village when he heard something odd amidst the chatter and general bustle of cars and crowds—tinny, droning, mechanical, an odd enough noise that Avery stopped and looked around in confusion.

The telephone box, red, cast iron, the glass panes covered with moisture from the recent snowfall and almost opaque was emitting a noise. The telephone inside it was definitely ringing.

Avery frowned at it, trying to remember how they worked. He was quite certain that, in the event of a ringing phone, someone was supposed to pick it up, but the box was empty. No one but he stood anywhere near it.

When the ringing stopped, he shrugged and kept walking.

Then the ringing started again.

He stopped and it started yet again, seeming to pick up intensity.

Avery was good at many things. He had a sharper memory than Lucas, an ability to think with a clear head and competitiveness that made learning practical skills all too easy. However, when it came to leaving things alone...Avery had never been good at turning and walking away.

So when the phone started trilling for a sixth time, and still no one moved to pick it up, Avery cursed under his breath and stepped into the box. It took him a moment to figure out exactly what to do, before he raised the receiver to his ear.

Static crackled.

"Hello?" He felt silly, talking to nothing but his fragmented reflection in the glass panes. He was about to put it down and leave when the voice broke through the other line.

"Avery?" A pause. The voice sounded unsteady, like whoever it was had been crying. Or laughing, or shouting, or something else equally hysterical.

Avery stiffened.

"I'm going to need that favour."

Boundary
The Other Horizons Trilogy – Book One

Never try to open the locked doors. Never question what you are told. And never attempt to cross the Boundary.

Kept inside an eerie estate for their entire lives, Penny and her five friends have had no contact with the outside world, with their only windows being a handful of books, a sinister master and a secretive housekeeper.

Fed up with living a mystery, Penny begins breaking all the rules and finally tries to escape; but what she uncovers is far more devastating than she could have imagined. It rapidly becomes a deadly struggle for the truth in a world where nothing is what it seems, and friendship can be either your greatest weapon…or your biggest liability.

Lodestone Books
978-1-78279-918-4

LODESTONE BOOKS

Lodestone Books

YOUNG ADULT FICTION

Lodestone Books offers a broad spectrum of subjects in YA/
NA literature. Compelling reading, the Teen/Young/New Adult
reader is sure to find something edgy, enticing and innovative.
From dystopian societies, through a whole range of fantasy,
horror, science fiction and paranormal fiction, all the way to the
other end of the sphere, historical drama, steam-punk adventure,
and everything in between (including crime, coming of age and
contemporary romance). Whatever your preference you will
discover it here.
If you have enjoyed this book, why not tell other readers by
posting a review on your preferred book site. Recent bestsellers
from Lodestone Books are:

AlphaNumeric
Nicolas Forzy
When dyslexic teenager Stu accidentally transports himself into a
world populated by living numbers and letters, his arrival triggers
a prophecy that pulls two rival communities into war.
Paperback: 978-1-78279-506-3 ebook: 978-1-78279-505-6

Shanti and the Magic Mandala
F.T. Camargo
In this award-winning YA novel, six teenagers from around the world gather for a frantic chase across Peru, in search of a sacred object that can stop The Black Magicians' final plan.
Paperback: 978-1-78279-500-1 ebook: 978-1-78279-499-8

Time Sphere
A timepathway book
M.C. Morison
When a teenage priestess in Ancient Egypt connects with a school-boy on a visit to the British Museum, they each come under threat as they search for Time's Key.
Paperback: 978-1-78279-330-4 ebook: 978-1-78279-329-8

Bird Without Wings
FAEBLES
Cally Pepper
Sixteen-year-old Scarlett has had more than her fair share of problems, but nothing prepares her for the day she discovers she's growing wings...
Paperback: 978-1-78099-902-9 ebook: 978-1-78099-901-2

Briar Blackwood's Grimmest of Fairytales
Timothy Roderick
After discovering she is the fabled Sleeping Beauty, a brooding goth-girl races against time to undo her deadly fate.
Paperback: 978-1-78279-922-1 ebook: 978-1-78279-923-8